William McGonagall
– Freefall

William McGonagall
– Freefall

SPIKE MILLIGAN
and
JACK HOBBS

MICHAEL JOSEPH
LONDON

MICHAEL JOSEPH

Published by the Penguin Group
27 Wrights Lane, London W8 5TZ
Viking Penguin Inc., 375 Hudson Street, New York, New York 10014, USA
Penguin Books Australia Ltd, Ringwood, Victoria, Australia
Penguin Books Canada Ltd, 10 Alcorn Avenue, Toronto, Ontario, Canada M4V 3B2
Penguin Books (NZ) Ltd, 182–190 Wairau Road, Auckland 10, New Zealand

Penguin Books Ltd, Registered Offices: Harmondsworth, Middlesex, England

First published in Great Britain 1992

Typeset by DatIX International Limited, Bungay, Suffolk
Typeset in 12/14 pt Palatino
Printed in England by Clays Ltd, St Ives plc

A CIP catalogue record for this book is available from the British Library

ISBN 0 7181 3665 9

THE PRIME MINISTER'S
SEX CHANGE

He rose from his Louis Quinze bed and wondered what it was doing in the YMCA. The sign had said, 'Louise Quinze and Lodgings 2/6d a night'. Louise Quinze wasn't there so he had to sleep alone. The Pinkerton Agency had hired him to find out why the Prime Minister of England had undergone a sex change after a vote in Parliament.

Mrs Thatcher had overnight and overwrought disappeared from Number Ten and reappeared as Mr Major.

'SEX CHANGE MINISTER TAKES OVER ENGLAND', said the *Sun*.

'NEW PRIME MINISTER REVEALS HERSELF TO BE A MAN', said *The Times*.

'I'm not voting for her again until she gets rid of it,' said Mrs Gladys Threats, a widow from Lewisham. 'I'm glad my husband Dick is not alive to see it; mind you, he didn't see much of it when he *was* alive, but there you go,' she said, pointing to the outside toilet.

Meanwhile, William McGonagall, private dick (he always carried one) commenced his search for the missing Prime Minister, his socks, his underpants and other sex aids. First he would search No 10a. It was a shock when told by the duty policeman, 'I'm sorry sir, there's no 10a Downing Street.' McGonagall switched on his Dick Tracy Radio Watch. Alas, the battery was low. None of this daunted McGonagall. He knew one thing, the time! 'Och, Constable,

5

it's ten-thirty. Do ye nae realise that Mrs Thatcher has turned into a man with extra parts?'

'This is all news to me,' said the policeman blowing his whistle.

'Och,' said McGonagall. 'There's no need to make a fool of yourself, what about you and Miss Greta Thighs of Streatham?'

'That is a lie,' said the constable. 'I thought she was over sixteen. I was only twelve and had to stand on an orange box.'

'You're nae much of a policeman,' said McGonagall.

'I'm as much of a policeman as I can be,' said the policeman, giving his truncheon a good shake. There was a screech of brakes, a white Mercedes came to a halt. Out leapt the manager of the YMCA. He flashed a bill stamped 'OVERDUE'.

'I'm not overdue,' said McGonagall. 'I'm over here.'

'That's no good to me,' said the manager. 'I want this bill paid in a month.'

'Right, how about December?' said McGonagall.

'How about December?' said the policeman.

'Look,' said McGonagall. 'Stick to policing.'

'And talking of the Bill,' said the policeman, 'I've been in it seven years.'

'And you look every inch a policeman with a fine truncheon,' said the enraged manager, then 'December is eight months away,' he continued.

'It's perfect timing,' said McGonagall. 'Ten thirty-five.' During these moments McGonagall's radio watch spoke.

'Say, McGonagall buddy, have you found the missing Prime Minister?'

'No!' said McGonagall, whose wit never failed him.

Apropos of nothing the policeman said, 'You're a fine-looking Scotsman.'

'Aye, it just goes to show,' said McGonagall and showed just a bit.

All this while England had no Prime Minister of any known sex. 'We'll have to settle for a bisexual,' said the Leader of the House of Lords and they put it to the vote. There were eighteen spoilt papers, the dirty devils. The strain on McGonagall was immense. He was convinced he could recognise a nude female Prime Minister at ten paces, as he could a nude male, but! a fully clothed bisexual would baffle him.

'Och,' he said fluently. 'Clothing, one of the world's cunningest disguises.'

'I'm going off duty now,' said the constable, with a great blast on his whistle. His teeth flew out.

The manager of the YMCA knew at last that he had met his match. He found it in a small box in his pocket. McGonagall focused his X-ray gaze between 10 and 11 Downing Street. Using his right hand to push them back in, pausing to insert a suppository, he renewed his search.

'Taxi,' he shouted, raising his right hand with the index finger extended.

'This is not a taxi,' said the driver. 'It is a 15b bus going to Catford.'

'That's good,' said McGonagall. 'There's a man in Reykjavik I want to interview.'

'Look,' said the bus driver. 'I don't go anywhere near Reykjavik, it's bad enough having to go via Clapham Common.'

'There, there,' said McGonagall, consolingly, patting him on the right shoulder, the hip, the knee, the ankle and the instep. 'I'm looking for the lost Prime Minister.'

'Well, you won't find him on 'ere,' said the bus driver. 'It's bad enough going via Clapham Common without hiding a Prime Minister.'

'I want this bill paid in a month'

'What's your name?' said McGonagall. The driver paused to think. 'Dr Watson,' he said finally.

'Och,' said McGonagall. 'What a good memory. A doctor, eh? Have you got a plague on board?'

'No,' said the bus driver. 'We've got rid of the plague, he got off at Tottenham. All we've got left are bronchitis and piles, take your choice.'

'That's very big of you,' said McGonagall, 'and you're a fine sight for any passenger to see.'

'Fares please,' said a voice. In a flash McGonagall was under the seat along with the bus driver. It was the start of a life-long partnership that was to last over an hour.

'What would you say,' said McGonagall, 'about becoming my partner in a search for an unidentified Prime Minister?'

'What would I say?' queried the bus driver. 'I would say expenses and all found. Dr Watson got bus expenses but he didn't find much though he searched McGonagall thoroughly.'

'Och,' said McGonagall. It was the start of a life-long partnership that had already lasted a quarter of an hour.

'You say,' said Dr Watson, searching McGonagall for expenses, 'you are looking for a missing Prime Minister.'

'Yes, I remember saying that,' said McGonagall. 'How nice of you to remember.'

Dr Watson peered into a microscope at the fingerprints.

'I found these on the doorknob in your office,' he said.

'Whose are they?' said McGonagall with a puzzled frown.

'They're yours,' said Watson.

'That's solved the mystery,' said McGonagall.

'Tell me,' said Dr Watson, adjusting his Homburg, 'why do you have that rope ladder hanging from the first-floor window?'

'It's for those people trying to avoid the doorknob. We should never join the EEC – we don't want a frog on the throne of England,' said McGonagall.

'Aye, yes,' said Dr Watson. 'It's bad enough having the Queen.'

'It would be terrible for Prince Philip,' said McGonagall.

'Did you know that the frog is near to extinction?' said Watson, gobbing out of the window.

'Aye,' said McGonagall. 'So are Prince Philips.'

'You mean we are down to our last Prince Philip?' said Watson.

'Yes,' said McGonagall.

'You've turned out a fine Scotsman,' said Dr Watson.

'Really?' said McGonagall. 'Who was he?'

Rather than answer, Watson feigned death.

'Where would you look for the Prime Minister of England?' said McGonagall.

'Everywhere,' said Watson.

'That's a good place,' said McGonagall adjusting his kilt and finding immediate relief. 'That was a good feign then, had me fooled.'

There was a silence as the two men contemplated. Dr Watson contemplated a shepherd's pie he had once operated on with the shepherd looking on. At the same time McGonagall contemplated Dick's Eel and Winkle stall where he had spent several holidays as a child.

'Och, I remember the smell of the winkles as they were dragged screaming from their shells in the fresh morning breeze, and Dick there with his mallet silencing them on their way.'

'Well, I'll just polish these handcuffs,' said Watson. 'You never know when we might meet a criminal with his wrists extended.'

'Personally,' said McGonagall, 'I've never met a man with extended wrists.'

'Well here comes one now,' said Watson. To their horror he was not a criminal, but an innocent wrist-extender passing by.

'That was a near thing,' said Dr Watson.

A feeling of utter helplessness swept over the canny Scot, so he did a highland fling.

'I *think* a good place to start looking would be the French Chamber of Deputies,' said Watson.

'The French Chamber?' said McGonagall. 'I never knew they used one.'

'Ah, yes,' said Watson, 'the last time I was here on holiday it was full to the brim.'

'Do you think our Prime Minister was involved?' said McGonagall.

'No, he was in Lewisham,' said Watson.

'That was just a disguise,' said McGonagall. 'He often disguises himself as Lewisham. I think it's a family tradition,' he said, and gobbed out of the window, which was one of his family traditions.

'You dirty bugger,' said a voice from below.

'That voice,' said McGonagall, 'I recognise that voice. That's Ned Sherrin, presenter, producer, wit and holder of a mortgage for twenty-five years.'

'Ahoy there, Ned,' said McGonagall.

Ned, who was covered in it, looked up.

'Are you the dirty bugger?' said Sherrin.

'Nae,' said McGonagall. 'I'm a different dirty bugger – you see, it's a tradition in his family and he's trying to keep it going.'

'Well, it's going all over me,' said Sherrin.

'And good luck with your twenty-five-year mortgage,' said McGonagall.

Watson gobbed out of the window again.

'So the tradition goes on,' said McGonagall.

Watson looked through his microscope searching the small print in *The Exchange and Mart*.

FOR SALE: black dog, will exchange for Swannee Whistle with Rolls Royce fingering.

11

'Och, oh dear,' said Watson. 'It's not like the good old days. I tried to exchange a set of Indian clubs for the Queen of Tahiti. Do you know what,' he added, 'I never got a single reply to that. In fact, I've still got the Indian clubs and Tahiti has still got the queen.'

'Is there any mention of the Prime Minister?' asked McGonagall, bowing low to ease one out.

'I've been reading *The Exchange and Mart* for forty years,' said Watson, 'and there ain't a lady living in the land as I'd swap for my dear old dutch.'

Despite the information from Dr Watson that there wasn't a lady living in the land that he'd swap for his dear old dutch, it didn't help in his search for the Prime Minister. Again McGonagall had no idea that Dr Watson had married a Dutch woman.

'Was it for her tulips?' he queried.

'No,' said Dr Watson. 'It was her ability to build dykes to prevent the flooding of the lowland marshes.'

'What a romantic affair it must have been,' said McGonagall. 'You with your Indian clubs and her with her dykes.'

'We weren't very happy – I had to leave her,' said Watson.

'Oh,' said McGonagall. 'What happened?'

'She flooded me,' said Watson.

'Aye, you're still damp,' said McGonagall.

'It didn't happen that long ago,' said Watson.

'I'm in two minds to know what to do,' said McGonagall.

'Which one are you in now?' said Watson.

'Lewisham,' said McGonagall.

'Oh, that one,' said Dr Watson, his eyes moist with tears.

ENCOUNTER WITH A
ROLLED TROUSER LEG

They booked on the Orient Express, a great pity as neither of them wanted to go anywhere. Hercule Poirot eyed the two men suspiciously. With great stealth he moved across the dining car.

'Gentlemen,' he commenced.

'Gentlemen,' repeated McGonagall. 'There must be some mistake. We are but humble third-class deck passengers on a cattle-boat bound for Panama.'

'Quelle brilliant disguise,' said Hercule Poirot. 'It is so perfect as to have almost fooled me.'

'Quelle surprise,' said McGonagall.

'If you insist,' said Poirot, showing them an identity card of the lady and the donkey.

'Ah, you're from the Sûreté,' said Watson. 'I've seen that donkey before in Port Said.'

'Ah, I can see you are a man of the world,' said Poirot.

'Where else?' said McGonagall.

Poirot had met his match.

'Vous comprendez the noo, England is without the Prime Minister for le moment?' said McGonagall.

'Personally, monsieur,' said Poirot, 'I don't give le fuck.'

'What about le Grand Alliance?' said Watson.

'I don't give le fuck about that either,' said Poirot.

'Refreshments,' said un passing waiter. Immediately Poirot rolled the leg of his trousers up.

'He's a Mason,' Poirot whispered, 'and this is the only way to get service.'

McGonagall, Watson and Poirot qualifying for croissants and chips

'That's funny,' said Watson, rolling up his trouser leg. 'Back home we have to use money.'

'Oh dear,' said McGonagall. 'In a kilt, under this system, I could starve to death.'

But McGonagall, ever ready for French cunning, pulled the string that released his spring-loaded trousers. In a flash he had rolled up one leg to Masonic height and ordered croissants and chips. The train thundered on through the French countryside.

'Sacré bleu,' said Hercule Poirot, 'not so loud! People will hear, such is the hatred of the English. French people are already trying to get off. Le driver is trying to get off with first-class passenger, Mlle Fifi, who has just returned from her triumphant tour with the donkey in Port Said.'

'It is all inclusive in Saga Pensioners' Holiday tour,' said Mlle Fifi. 'They are greatly refreshed by what they see.'

McGonagall heard this stimulating conversation and made himself known.

'You're a fine wee lassie and I like the work you're doing. The donkey sanctuary is eternally grateful to you.'

'Excuse me, ma'am,' said Dr Watson. 'Have you by any chance seen a British Prime Minister during your act?'

'Does he use binoculars?' said Mlle Fifi.

'No,' said Dr Watson, raising his Homburg and releasing a bald head.

'In that case, I haven't,' said Mlle Fifi.

'Oh, he wasn't in a case,' said Watson. 'He was a free-standing citizen.'

The train thundered through le French countryside.

'Tickets please,' said a voice.

In a flash, McGonagall and Watson were under the seats, renewing their friendship.

'What are you deux doing under this seat?' said a passenger from le working class.

'Le financial reasons,' said McGonagall, crawling out.

The train arrived in Paris dead on time. True to Grand French tradition the driver shot himself. They found a hotel called Danger Falling Masonry; in fact, three masons fell out of the window while they were there.

'We want a door with adjoining rooms,' said Dr Watson adjusting his Homburg.

'Have you any means of identification?' said the manager. McGonagall produced an apple.

'What is your name?' said the manager.

'Granny Smith,' said McGonagall. While the manager was recovering Watson handed him a banana.

'Fyfe is the name.'

There was no denying that these two men were masters of deception. It wasn't long before gendarmes were on their tail. There was a tap on the door; why the French built taps on doors was baffling.

'Who do you wish to see?' said McGonagall through the keyhole.

'Granny Smith and Mr Fyfe,' came the reply.

'Quick, the window,' said McGonagall. Watson knotted the bedsheets. As they slithered down, they met the manager coming up.

'I thought you might do something like this,' he said.

'So we did,' said McGonagall, and did it.

Later, they were given a night's refuge and frenzied scratching by a kindly gypsy who lent them his caravan under the proviso that they did not declare war on France.

'We'll do our best,' said McGonagall.

At four in the morning Watson woke the gypsy. 'I'm sorry to say, an hour ago McGonagall declared war on France but lost.'

'Oh, dear,' said the gypsy. 'Did it frighten my donkey?'

McGonagall approached.

'What's all this?' he said, climbing a tree. 'Can't anyone have a war without you telling everyone about it?' At which point he missed his hold, crashed to the ground and lay in a cloud of dust half unconscious.

'This should help,' said the gypsy, throwing a bucket of water over him.

'Hoi hup la,' he said, springing to his feet. 'I didn't know there were showers in the room.'

It was time for McGonagall to toss a caber.

'You'll not find a caber in France,' said Dr Watson.

'Just put your foot here,' said McGonagall; the next thing Watson knew he was hurtling, caber style, through the sweet French air, landing on his Homburg.

'I'm not used to this sort of thing,' he said.

'It takes time,' said McGonagall, who had never hurled a Dr Watson before.

'If there had been a caber handy I would never ha' done such a thing.'

'It's too late for apologies,' said Watson.

'No,' said McGonagall. 'It's only two o'clock. Just put yer tootsie in my hands here.' Again Watson found himself hurtling in the air, this time landing in the river. All this behaviour put a great strain on the relationship.

'Had a nice swim?' said McGonagall as Watson come dripping ashore.

'Och, there's nothing like a good laugh,' said McGonagall who was in a splendid mood. 'You're dripping,' he laughed.

'It's not dripping,' said Watson. 'It's water, dripping has an entirely different consistency.' A gendarme intervened.

'Excusez-moi, I arrest you for murder on the high seas,' he said, and made with his night stick.

'I was only swimming, Constable,' said Dr Watson.

'Well,' said the gendarme. 'I cannot arrest you for swimming, but I can arrest you for murder on the high seas.'

Watson squeezed out his hat. 'But I have never committed murder on the high seas,' he said.

'Oh dear,' said the gendarme, bursting into tears. 'That ruins my case.' McGonagall comforted the weeping man and his case.

'Are you sure you've never committed murder on the high seas?' he said. Watson shook his head.

'Never on the high seas,' he said. 'Or even on the high land.'

'Are you a foreigner?' said the gendarme.

'Only when I leave England,' said Watson.

'Have you any means of identification?' said the gendarme.

'Yes,' said Watson. 'I own a Bechstein piano.'

'That's not good enough,' said the gendarme.

'Very well,' said Watson, 'I'll buy a Yamaha.' This remark stunned the gendarme.

McGonagall meets Watson

To ease the tension McGonagall did handstands. In this position he sang the 'Battle Hymn of the Republic'.

'I can't see what good this is doing,' said Watson.

'Why is your friend exposing himself?' said the gendarme.

'Search me,' said Watson. The gendarme searched Watson and found the following: a bus ticket, a cigar, a postcard of the lady and the donkey, and an anti-aircraft gun. The last item puzzled the gendarme.

'Are you expecting an air-raid?' he said.

'We were fools to leave the Orient Express,' said McGonagall. 'Our luggage was on it.' He choked back a sob, his best tartan underwear, his applicator, and curried suppositories were in that luggage. They repaired to a men's wear shop in the Rue de Vale.

'Have you a pair of underpants, size 9?' he said.

'Oui,' said the salesman, 'but I'm wearing them.'

'Well, fuck you,' said McGonagall.

'Le insult,' said the salesman and drew his sword.

McGonagall and Watson were now running at speed pursued by the salesman. By nightfall they had shaken him off; McGonagall had often shaken off, but never a French underwear salesman. McGonagall paused to fill in a child allowance application — he hadn't got a child but there was no harm in trying. 'The woods are full of them,' he said. The man who heard him was a French postman on his rounds.

'I heard that,' he said. His name was, and still is, Pierre Mons Tonge — his father had named him after the Battle of Tonge.

'That's a silly name for a postman,' said McGonagall. 'He should be called Pierre Red Parcel delivery, I mean, who's ever heard of the Battle of Tonge?'

'I have,' said a woman of eighteen stone, dead weight, with cross eyes. 'I'm pleased to meet you,' said McGonagall, extending his hand.

'And you,' she said, shaking Dr Watson's. 'Yes, my grandfather was at the Battle of Tonge. It was a little known battle, it was so little my grandfather didn't know he'd been in it.'

'Who were they fighting?' said McGonagall. The woman took out a worn old photograph, it showed the manager of the mortgage department of the Bradford and Bingley.

'That's Dick Mocks,' said Watson snatching the photograph. 'He ran away with my wife and the fish knives,' he said, hitting and rehitting the photo, two straight lefts and an uppercut he gave it, then four right jabs, three blows to the chin, the solar plexus and a series of straight arm jabs.

'Stop,' said McGonagall restraining Watson. 'You're fading the photograph.'

The eighteen-stone, cross-eyed woman took the photo, pressed it to her cheek, kissed it, then set fire to it. They never saw her again but, in quiet moments, Watson would remember the photograph and beat the shit out of McGonagall all the while shouting 'That's Dick Mocks'. McGonagall regained consciousness and cautioned Watson with an iron bar. There was nothing for it but to hail a taxi. 'Sieg heil,' they said as taxi after taxi went by. Finally, a German one with a Nazi sign pulled up.

'Ach,' said the driver. 'It's good to hear the old songs. Where to?'

'Where's a good place?' said McGonagall.

'The Pink Elephant, Berlin,' said the driver spiel.

'If Hitler were alive today,' said the taxi driver, 'do you know what he would be doing?'

Dr Watson hazarded a guess. 'Dying?' he said.

'Apart from that,' said the driver spiel.

'Apart from that,' said Watson, 'I don't know, I give up, what would Hitler be doing?'

'How do I know?' said the enraged driver. 'I was asking *you*.'

The journey passed in silence save for the secret delivery of an occasional nether wind. Finally, the enraged driver broke the silence. 'I think if Hitler were alive today he would be doing the Karzi, he was a very good painter, he stopped to declare war on Poland.'

'My great-grandmother came from Poland,' said Watson.

'Well, they've all got to come from somewhere,' said McGonagall crossing and recrossing his legs in a rhythmic manner. This all ceased when his X-ray gaze focused on the taxi meter. Despite twenty prayers to St Jude, patron saint of the poor, nothing could stop the meter ticking up the price.

'Thirty deutschmarks,' said the driver spiel.

'Where are we going to find that sort of money?' gasped McGonagall.

'Germany,' said the driver. 'Anyone will take it.'

'Does that include you?' said McGonagall.

Seeing McGonagall was nigh to financial collapse, Watson drew on his medical knowledge. 'This man is bankrupt,' he said, putting his stethoscope to his friend's chest. 'I won't charge you for the visit,' he said, taking McGonagall's pulse and putting it in his pocket.

'Tell me, doc, am I going to live?' asked McGonagall.

'Yes, you're going to live at the YMCA.'

'Vot is zer matter vid your friend?' said the taxi driver.

'He has Hodgkinson's disease, and Hodgkinson has his. It is a fear of taxi meters.'

'The White Elephant,' said the taxi driver.

'I thought it was pink,' said Watson.

'It's turned out to be a white one; that's the manager out there,' said the taxi driver, pointing to a man in rags with a begging bowl. 'Vot a tragic figure.'

'Wait till you see mine,' said McGonagall, shading his eyes from the meter.

'Where is my fare?' demanded the taxi driver.

'Would you believe it,' said Dr Watson. 'It's in a tea caddy on my mantelpiece at 6 Krill Street, Neasden.'

'You vant me to go to London to get mein fare, do you think I'm mad?'

'Yes,' said the doctor. 'My fee for this visit is five guineas.'

The taxi raced away to Neasden. To ease the tension McGonagall opened a door in the street. There was the sound of gunfire.

SIMPLE CAMEL MASSAGE – AN EXPERIENCE

'Bang, bang and welcome to the 8th Army,' said General Montgomery,

'Are you in the Highland column?'

'No, the obituary column,' said McGonagall.

Montgomery put on a medal. 'Stand by for my star attraction, El Alamein.'

At this Dr Watson took up a heroic pose and said, 'That battle was fought in 1943.'

'Yes,' said Monty. 'This is an encore for BBC television. In fact, we were waiting for Terry Wogan for the start.'

Montgomery put on a fresh medal.

'Ha' ye gotta banjo?' said McGonagall.

'Only a military one,' said Monty handing it across. There and then McGonagall sang 'The Battle of Alamein'.

'I've never heard it sung better,' said Montgomery. At that moment the banjo exploded.

'Damn,' said Montgomery, looking at the blasted figure.

McGonagall playing an explosive banjo

'The Germans must have mined it, never mind, you've won the MM for gallantry.'

He fixed a medal to the blasted figure.

'My, you look fine,' he said. The blasted figure said, 'Ha' you any Horlicks?'

'No. No Horlicks,' said Montgomery, 'But I have *a* Horlick.'

McGonagall took the Horlick. It exploded. 'Blast, that's been mined as well,' said Montgomery. 'Here are two tickets to see the famous belly dancer, Mrs Saida Bint.'

'I've nay ever seen a belly dance. Will I go blind?' he said.

As he mounted a camel, it exploded.

'I don't believe it!' said Montgomery.

'I do,' said McGonagall, thirty feet up in the air and on his way down. He fell at Montgomery's feet.

'Welcome to Egypt,' he said.

'You're welcome to it,' said McGonagall.

'Come, effendi,' said the camel boy. 'Your camel's getting cold.' Soon McGonagall and Watson were seated twixt the humps. As camels go it wasn't bad, except when it did go, it was all over Watson. The camel boy was hitting McGonagall and the camel alternately.

'Can you leave me out of this?' said McGonagall.

'I'm sorry, effendi,' said the camel boy. 'I've never been able to tell the difference between a Scotsman, a camel and Cliff Richard.'

'Ooh,' said McGonagall, under a hail of blows. 'You should see an optician.' So off went the camel boy to see Cliff Richard.

'Can you drive one of these things?' said McGonagall.

'Yes,' said Watson. 'Just give me the string, you massage the humps.'

With string and hump massage our heroes continued.

'This is no way to spend Christmas,' said McGonagall.

'Christmas?' said Watson. 'This is August.'

'I still say this is no way to spend Christmas,' said McGonagall; a bullet whizzed past his head.

'Halt, who goes there?' said a voice.

'I do,' said McGonagall. 'But most of it is in my under-pants.'

'Advance and be recognised.' It was a soldier from the Irish Fusiliers.

'I'm sorry, I don't recognise either of you,' he said.

'We don't recognise either of you either,' said McGonagall.

'Pass, friends,' said the Fusilier. 'And a Merry Christmas.'

With string pulling and hump massage our heroes continued

'You see?' said McGonagall. 'I'm not the only one.'

'God, that sun's hot,' said Watson.

'Then don't touch it,' said McGonagall. 'It was a surprise to me,' he added.

'What was?' said Watson.

'Your grandmother coming from Poland.'

'It was for me too,' said Watson. 'The only time I saw her she was coming from Lewisham.'

McGonagall gasped. 'Lewisham,' he said in wonder. 'The golden city,' and went into a poem.

Oh, tis such a great pity
That we are not in Lewisham city,
'Tis a place I want to be,
But it is a long way from the sea,
That is why you don't see any ships of the line,
Otherwise everything is really fine!
I wish I could be in Lewisham.
Then I could say definitely, here-I-am.

'Three out of ten,' said Watson as he wiped away a tear. 'That was very moving.'

'It's more than I could say for the camel,' said McGonagall in a fever of hump massage. Watson shielded his eyes from the sun, he recalled seeing this done before with good results.

'I think I see ahead, a mirage.'

'Make up your mind — is it a mirage or a head?' said McGonagall.

'It's hard to say,' said Watson.

'Then don't say it,' said McGonagall.

'Ahoy,' said a sunburned sailor. 'Have you seen the HMS *Brongle*?'

'Quick,' said McGonagall. 'Say Hello sailor.'

'I was rowing the longboat,' said the sunburned sailor. 'After a few minutes it sank.'

'Och,' said McGonagall. 'That's not very long for a long boat.'

'Never mind that,' said the sunburned sailor. 'Can you give me a lift?'

McGonagall said, 'We haven't got a lift, we've only got a camel.'

'Come aboard me hearty,' said Watson. With the hearty aboard they were off.

'Have you ever been in the Navy?' said the hearty.

'No,' said McGonagall. 'Have I missed something?'

'You missed the sailor's hornpipe round and round the windlass.'

'Oh dear,' said McGonagall who was filled with gloom.

'Cheer up,' said the hearty, and gave him a Fisherman's Friend.

'I don't remember being in the Navy,' said Watson, 'but I quite clearly remember being in John Bell & Croydons.'

'Oh,' said the sailor. 'Did you do the hornpipe?'

'No, I only went there for some lung syrup. I could have done the hornpipe I suppose,' he said, 'but I don't think it would have gone down very well.'

'Oh,' said the hearty tying a few knots.

'The lung syrup went down well,' said Watson. The camel and its passengers were now in the shadow of the Pyramids.

'The kings of Egypt are buried under them,' said Watson.

'No wonder,' said McGonagall, 'the weight must have killed them.' Watson agitated the string on the camel to try and improve its performance, he only wished he could have improved his own. They approached a bazaar on the outskirts of Cairo.

'Hey, Mister Thatcher,' shouted a reeking Arab vendor. 'You want to sell camel?'

'What will you give us for it?' said the wily McGonagall.

'A saddle,' said the Arab.

'Done,' said McGonagall. Using the instruction book our heroes slithered to the ground and missed.

From here on they travelled by saddle.

LAND IS SIGHTED

'We've landed in Lewisham again,' said Watson, 'I recognise the bottle bank.'

'That's nae good to me,' said McGonagall, 'I lost my bottle years ago.'

'What we need is money,' said Watson. Holding out his hat he started to sing. McGonagall was doing an energetic highland fling. 'Money will soon start rolling in,' he said.

'You know what someone just put in my hat?' said Watson. 'A dirty big bald head.' The sailor stood mutely by tying a few knots in his appendages. How he yearned for HMS *Brongle*. By midday they had arrived back at McGonagall's London office. A big surprise for the readers.

'Miss Moneypenny, I'm back!'

'Where have you come from?' she said. With a wily grin McGonagall tapped his nose – fortunately nothing fell out.

'The other side of this door,' he said. Miss Moneypenny phoned the morticians. 'Cancel the wreath, the coffin was empty, he's just come in.'

'Any messages while I was away?' he said.

'This arrived from Downing Street.' She handed him a parcel. Using their combined strength McGonagall and Watson tore it open.

'It's a Get-Well sock,' said McGonagall. 'I don't understand, none of my legs are ill.' Watson put it under his microscope.

'Perhaps they think I'm one-legged,' said McGonagall, pulling the sock over his head. 'How do I look?' he said.

Watson told him. A knock at the door, no sooner entered Admiral of the Fleet Edward Noffs.

'That sailor,' he said, pointing a fish at the hearty, 'is from the HMS *Brongle*. We've been missing him and his hornpiping.' The sailor fell weeping at the Admiral's gold braid epaulette, tears pouring down into the Admiral's boots, with every step little squirts of water shot from the lace holes. Arm in arm they stood singing 'Rule Britannia'. McGonagall and Watson both helped by giving them glasses of salt water with fish in.

'I'll remember those screams to my dying day,' said Watson putting on a shroud. There entered a large black man called Martin Squills carrying a tuba. He circled McGonagall three times oompa-pa-ing. 'Look out, it's a Tubagram,' said Miss Moneypenny. Quickly Watson wedged the tuba over the man's head.

'Are you all right in there?' said McGonagall through the mouthpiece.

'Yes, wot am de weather like out dere?'

McGonagall told him it was raining with gale force winds. 'You're in the best place,' he said.

'Do you know who I am?' said the occupant of the tuba. Here was a man in a tuba who didn't know who he was.

'Can't you remember?' said McGonagall through the mouthpiece. 'I'll have to take you to the police.'

The police looked up the tuba but didn't recognise the man. 'He's not on our list of wanted men,' they said.

'You mean this personage is unwanted?' said McGonagall.

'That is true. In fact, he's the most unwanted man on our list.'

McGonagall took the man in the tuba outside and let him go in the street.

'The dirty devil,' moaned the great crowd.

'Dat's my husband in dere,' said a coloured lady, inserting herself up the tuba. The four-legged tuba walked up Whitehall.

'I want that act,' said Lord Delfont from his stretched Rolls Royce. 'Stop here,' he said to his stretched chauffeur. 'Who is their manager?'

'I am,' said McGonagall.

'You don't look as if you can manage,' said Lord Delfont.

'Well, so far I've managed on ten pounds a week,' said McGonagall.

'Sign here,' said Lord Delfont, pointing to an IOU.

'Wait, this looks like a trick,' said McGonagall.

'It's not a trick. If I could do tricks I'd be on the stage,' said Lord Delfont.

'I'll not sign that until I see a lawyer,' said McGonagall. Lord Delfont handed him a telescope.

'Look up at that window.' Sure enough, through the telescope he could see Sir David Napley. At the Royal Command Performance, the four-legged tuba didn't go down well. All the Queen could hear was 'Someone get us out of dis bloody thing'.

'Get them off!' shouted Lord Delfont. Many chorus girls did so but McGonagall kept cool. Doing a soft shoe, he steered the four-legged tuba off the stage to boos from the audience and a hail of rotten eggs and tomatoes.

'Och, a true vegetarian,' he said, spattered with egg on his face.

Back at the office Miss Moneypenny and Watson had lunch off him, then boiled his kilt for soup. He sat shivering by the window, then by the door next to the cupboard.

'Variety is the splice of life,' he said.

'You mean spice,' said Watson.

'You mean bastard,' said McGonagall. 'You ate every tomato and egg off me, then gave me a bill for dry cleaning.' In came General Montgomery.

'Ah, there you are.' Sure enough, there he was. 'I've been looking for you, I hear you have a wonderful stage act called Flanagan and Allen. I want them to entertain the 8th Army and help me win World War Two.' McGonagall told him that he had Flanagan and Allen but they were stuffed up a tuba.

'Can't you unstuff them?' said Montgomery.

'No. General Rommel would see that one of them was Jewish and bomb him,' said McGonagall. 'It would ruin the act,' he said. Montgomery cocked a snook at McGonagall, who caught it.

'I'll have it dry frozen,' he said.

'Hands up,' said Montgomery pointing the 8th Army at him. 'Hand back that cocked snook, it has great sentimental value, it belonged to my mother.' In desperation McGonagall raised his kilt. At that very moment a photographer looking for a sensational story flashed his camera. It made headlines in the *News of the World.* 'SCOTSMAN SNOOKS A COCK AT GENERAL MONTGOMERY.' Seeing the photo the General went green with envy, red with anger, then white with rage. He published McGonagall's measurements in part two orders. When the Highland division read them they cheered McGonagall to the rafters, and he received many offers of marriage.

'I've worn this shroud for three days,' said Watson. 'And I'm not dead yet!'

'Patience,' said Miss Moneypenny.

McGonagall paced the floor. Watson followed in his shroud fighting off morticians. One mortician, a Mr Len Drench, pleaded, 'Please die, sir, business is bad, my wife and I are starving.'

'Would you give me a decent burial?' said Watson.

'Bury you?' said the mortician. 'We wouldn't bury you, we'd eat you.'

'Stop prodding my friend with that fork,' said McGonagall. 'You'll let the air out.'

31

A blind man approached. 'Can you see me across the road?' he said. McGonagall looked across the road. 'I'm looking across the road but there's no sign of you there.'

'I'll never get across at this rate,' said the blind man.

'Oh, what rate are you on?' said McGonagall.

'Thirty p. an hour,' said the blind man.

'Och, you must be rolling in it,' said McGonagall, searching the blind man for his wallet.

'Oh, McGonagall,' said Watson. 'How can you stoop so low?'

'Because he keeps his money in his sock.' At that moment his Dick Tracy watch came to life. 'Are you there?' it said.

'No, I'm here,' said McGonagall.

'Who is talking?' said the voice.

'You are,' said McGonagall. The voice was that of President Bush.

'Any movement on the missing Prime Minister?' McGonagall admitted he'd made several moves — mostly to avoid bailiffs.

'Where is Mrs Thatcher?' said Bush.

'Prepare yourself for a blow,' said McGonagall. 'People say she's in Dulwich.'

'As bad as that?' said Bush.

'Aye,' said McGonagall. 'There's a deposit on the house.'

'Is it pigeons?' said Bush.

'Aye,' said McGonagall.

'What about your eye?' said Bush.

'Aye is a Scottish word, Mr President,' said McGonagall.

'Rubbish, eye is an English word; everyone has two of them. I should know.'

The conversation was stopped by a war in Cambodia and dandruff. Dandruff is a scalp condition, a lot of people haven't got it. Likewise a lot of people haven't got a war in Cambodia. Fortunately, McGonagall only had dandruff, whereas war affects the whole body, dandruff only affects the scalp. 'I'm lucky I have nae got a Cambodian war of the scalp,' said McGonagall.

Using hired bicycles McGonagall and Watson rode back to the office.

Alas, both men crashed into a Chelsea pensioner, the old soldier and his gnarled walking stick lay prostrate on the pedestrian crossing. 'Och, old soldier and gnarled walking stick, I'm sorry.' The pensioner raised his head.

'You're sorry,' he said. 'Listen, I died in the last war for people like you,' then fainted. McGonagall quickly unscrewed his brandy flask and took a long drink.

'Ah, he looks better now,' he said.

'So do you,' said Watson, dialling fire, police and ambulance. Soon, supervised by the police, the fire brigade put the pensioner out with a deluge of hoses. Finally, arrived the ambulance with a stretcher and stretched the pensioner to ten feet six.

Back at the office a stranger was waiting, he was dressed like a Hindu and was.

'I'm from the Foreign Office,' he said.

'Aye, you look foreign,' said McGonagall, screwing back his brandy top. It was the first screw he'd had that year. Ah, yes, he recalled, i.e. Doris Draws, the one-legged beauty from Balham. He had played Prince Charming to her Cinderella at the town hall. Could anyone forget that size 14 glass slipper and the three-in-one oil to get it on?

'How?' said the Hindu from the Foreign Office, 'how at a time like this can you be so cheerful?'

Miss Moneypenny intervened. 'They are cheerful because they are cheery men who always smile when they are down, they always look on the bright side, they grin and

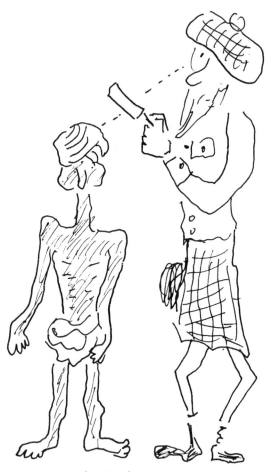

This Hindu is genuine

bear it, with a smile and a song they banish gloom, they laugh away dull care.'

'What a load of crap,' said the Hindu. Watson put the Hindu under the microscope.

'This Hindu is genuine,' he said. 'He is full of curry to bursting point, the only fingerprints are those of Mrs Doris Draws in his loin cloth.' So, thought McGonagall, Mrs

Doris Draws had been unfaithful to him. Never mind, there were other Hindus. With a sickening smile, a wink and a thumbs-up he said, 'Never mind, Hindu, there's lots more fish in the sea. Now get out.' The game was up and the Hindu knew it; he broke down. Slowly McGonagall and Watson jacked him up. He admitted he was an illegal Hindu immigrant and was scorbutic.

'Scorbutic. What does that mean?' said McGonagall. Then out of the blue, Watson said, 'What does it mean?' Miss Moneypenny stood and spoke through a loud hailer. 'Scorbutic, pertaining to, like or affected with scurvy.'

'We don't want to catch it,' said McGonagall hiding in a cupboard.

'Neither did I,' said the Hindu following him in.

'Look, leave a pound on the table and we won't tell on you,' said McGonagall. With certain movements from his religion, the Hindu made a deposit on the desk and withdrew.

'Did he leave a pound?' said McGonagall, reappearing.

'In curry powder,' said Watson. 'The Asiatic swine has deceived us by spelling the wrong word.' They gave the curry to the cat; the cat did sixty miles an hour round the room, shot through the cat flap and hit an old lady. (*Itma* 1939 Joke of the year.)

'I'm sorry, ma'am,' said McGonagall, bowing low.

'That's no bloody good,' said the old lady. 'That cat hit me in the fanny and it hasn't been used for fifty years.'

'A Merry Christmas to you both,' said McGonagall, touching his forelock, releasing a shower of dandruff. 'See, it's snowing.'

'It's not Christmas yet you silly man,' said the old lady. 'This is only October.'

'Och, then a merry October to you, ma'am,' said McGonagall.

'It's very hard crossing the road here,' said the old lady.

'There's a zebra crossing further up,' said McGonagall.

'I hope he's having more luck than me,' said the old lady. Now, McGonagall and Watson took the train to Istanbul. They examined the clues, no stone was left unturned; it was with surprise one morning that the citizens of Istanbul found every stone in the city had been turned.

Returning to London they found the great crowd in their street and a coalman halfway up a rope ladder.

'I'm delivering 'arf a ton of best nuts you ordered for Christmas.'

'It's only October,' said McGonagall.

'A merry October,' said the coalman climbing up. Arriving on the scene, Watson put the best nuts under the microscope.

'These are monkey nuts.'

'How do monkey nuts keep you warm?' enquired McGonagall.

'Carry 'em up and down this ladder! That will be five pounds.' Weeping, McGonagall unscrewed a five pound note from his wallet and started to poem:

> Oh, how terrible to have to pass him money,
> A sight that is not very funny.
> Goodbye lovely five pounds:
> I'll nae more hear your crinkling sounds.

Chanting the death march from Saul he slowly closed his wallet before pulling the bolts shut. Just then, three men burst into the room. McGonagall mopped it up.

'We are from the FBI,' they said in concert.

'Ah yes, here's a donation,' Watson said, passing them a monkey nut.

One FBI man stepped forward. 'I'm Steve Thudds, here

is my card.' Watson put it under his microscope. 'This is the ace of spades,' he said.

'Yes, I'm in disguise, see.' He removed his false beard, false nose, his false wig, his false ears, his teeth. Finally, he wasn't there.

'Fooled you,' said the second FBI man. 'I'm Dick Tracy.'

'Och, I've got one of your radio watches. I'll go in the toilet and we can have a two-way conversation.' From the toilet McGonagall said, 'Hello, Dick Tracy?'

'Hello, William McGonagall?' said Dick Tracy. 'Come out, we know you're in there.' McGonagall came out soaked.

'It was a blind man, he did nae know I was in there.' The FBI men became very serious.

'That's the man we are after, he's Dennis the Widdler, he only pretends to be blind and widdles on people. Usually he does it from a great height. He loves skyscrapers. We came to England to get away from him.'

The triumphant laughter of Dennis the Widdler came echoing up the stairway.

'Quick, go after him,' said Dick Tracy. McGonagall rushed to the toilet and went after him.

'I cannae see the sense of this,' he said, and rushed back and hid in the cupboard.

Dick Tracy opened the cupboard.

'Look, let's stop this silly game,' he said. McGonagall stopped the silly game.

'I was trying to keep up the dramatic tension like James Blonde,' said McGonagall.

'You mean Bond,' said Watson.

'You mean bastard,' said McGonagall. Dick Tracy held up a nude photograph of the Queen. McGonagall realised that the *News of the World* would give a million pounds for it. McGonagall snatched the photo, spread royal butter on it and ate it.

'God, you're clever,' said the stunned Tracy.

'Anything to save our Queen,' said Watson.

'Now,' said McGonagall. 'We have something over you Americans. The inside-leg measurement of Barbara Bush.' The information shook Tracy and several bits fell off.

'This is a fine bit,' said McGonagall, and picking it up he gave it to the cat.

THE LONE WOLF SALOON, TEXAS

An old crazed trapper was miming a Ragtime tune on an old crazed piano. In came a fresh-faced kid called William McGonagall.

'What're you drinking, kid?' said the barman.

'Nothing, can't you see?' said McGonagall.

'I heard that,' said six-gun Killer McGee.

'Go for your guns.'

'Och, they're back at the hotel, I'll go and get them,' said McGonagall.

'The hotel?' snarled Killer McGee. 'Don't give me that.'

McGonagall explained that he wasn't going to give him a hotel. McGee drew four of his six guns, fired them in all directions and back again. Those left standing carried on dancing.

'People like you make me sick,' said McGee into a bucket.

Suddenly there was a shooting. 'Duck behind the bar,' said the barman. McGonagall dived behind then stood up.

'There is no duck behind this bar,' he said. 'It's a chicken.'

'Are you calling me a liar?' snarled the barman.

'No, I'm calling this a chicken,' said McGonagall.

'That's fightin' talk,' said the barman.

'Step outside and say that,' said McGonagall. The barman stepped outside.

'That got rid of him,' said McGonagall.

'Listen my son,' said Doc Watson.

'I don't want to listen, to your son,' said McGonagall, 'he's got Crones disease – and Crones got his.'

The sound of a tremendous fight outside stopped. In came the barman with no teeth and two black eyes. 'Let that be a lesson to you,' he said to McGonagall.

'I wasn't out there,' said McGonagall.

'I'm glad you weren't,' said the barman. 'It was bad enough without you.'

'Any more requests?' cried the crazed pianist.

'Yes,' said a drunken voice. 'Stop playing the fucking piano.' But they still went on dancing. The saloon went quiet as the sound of a silver female voice was heard approaching. As a mark of respect they hid the spittoons. There entered through the swing doors a Salvation Army lass.

'Jesus loves me,' she trilled as the swing doors laid her flat.

'Well, he's the only one who does,' said a voice.

Spitting out teeth she leapt to her feet and rattled her tambourine. 'Give for the poor of the parish,' she said.

'Goddammit,' they moaned. 'We are the poor of the parish.'

'Have you nothing else to say?' she said, sidestepping a gob from the crazed pianist.

'Tigernuts,' said Killer McGee.

'Tigernuts?' she said. 'That doesn't mean much to me.'

'Well it means a lot to a tiger,' said Killer McGee, sidestepping a gob from the crazed Salvation Army girl.

'You've insulted a lady,' said fresh-faced McGonagall, drawing a pistol. 'I'm going to have to kill you.'

'Ha, ha,' said McGee. 'That's a water pistol.'

'Yes,' said McGonagall. 'I'm going to drown you.'

'Ah,' sang the refreshed Salvation Army girl. 'Jesus loves me.'

'He changed his mind then,' said McGonagall. The Salvation Army girl blushed to the roots of her hair.

'Has anyone told you that you're lovely?' said the fresh-faced McGonagall.

'No,' she said.

'Well, I think they got it right,' said McGonagall. Meanwhile the rough cowboys went on dancing with each other.

The curfew tolled the knell of parting day, the lowing herd passed slowly o'er the lea, and still they danced in

The Stoned Ranger

spite of it. Meanwhile, McGonagall revealed his true identity. A white Stetson and black mask with no eyeholes.

'It's the Stoned Ranger,' moaned the cowboys, cowering
in the spittoon. He backed towards the door, making
eyeholes as he went.

'Eyeholes,' said the rough cowboys.

'Nobody move,' he cried. With house prices at an all-time low, nobody dared, least of all rough dancing cowboys who had it all in the Bradford and Bingley. With a cry of 'Heigh ho Silver' McGonagall leapt on his white horse and off the other side.

'Upsadaisy,' said Tonto, his fantastic Indian friend.

With a cry of 'Heigh ho Upsadaisy', McGonagall was in the saddle and squashed them flat.

'White man scream with forked tongue,' said Tonto the fantastic.

'It's nae easy, Jamie,' said one of the squashed things.

'Heigh ho Silver, let's mosey.'

'This must be Indian territory,' said Hi Ho McGonagall as they passed Mr Patel's corner shop.

'Do you do takeaways?' said Hi Ho McGonagall.

'Yes, I do every kind of takeaway,' said Mr Patel, taking away McGonagall's wallet.

'I wouldn't do that if I were you,' said Hi Ho McSilver.

'Well, I'm not you and I've done it,' said Mr Patel, and was off.

With a screech of brakes the YMCA coach drew up in a cloud of dust, flies and dung. The YMCA manager, brandishing an unpaid bill, stepped into it.

'White man in heap trouble,' said Tonto as the manager slowly sank into it. They passed the time of day.

'Four-forty,' said McGonagall.

'Half past two,' said the man in it. 'I'm looking for the man with the money to pay this bill.'

'So am I,' said McGonagall pointing to a Patel disappearing over the horizon.

'Is that McGonagall?' said the man in it.

'He is now,' said McGonagall.

'Me lose track of story,' said the baffled Tonto with his ear to the ground.

'What can you hear?' said McGonagall.

'Me hear you say "What can you hear?"' said Tonto. 'Eagle overhead, bad medicine for white man.'

'Why?' said Mc Hi Ho McGonagall.

'He just crapped on you,' said Tonto. Colonel Custer and the twelfth cavalry reined to a halt. They too were covered in it.

'I see the eagle got you too,' said Custer.

'Some people say it's lucky,' said McGonagall.

'Not any more,' said Custer and shot it. Three puffs of smoke rose from a distant hill.

'Look Tonto,' said Hi Ho McGonagall. Tonto strained his eyes.

'Old Holborn,' he said.

'Sounds like lung trouble to me,' said Colonel Custer. 'I must be off.'

'All right, b . . . off,' said McGonagall.

'I'm away to Little Big Horn,' said Custer.

'The fool,' thought McGonagall. He started to poem:

Ooooooh 'twas wonderful to see Colonel Custer
With all the John Waynes he could muster,
To face up to a Chief called Sitting Bull
Who already had his hands full.
But when the battle started Custer did retreat a bit.
For out of him Sitting Bull did beat the shit.
When Mrs Custer heard of the tragedy
She cashed in Custer's Life Insurance Policy.

The Stoned Ranger and Tonto rode on. A strange-looking couple. McGonagall in a Stetson and kilt, with Tonto in a beret and knee-length evening dress. Many raiding Indians mistook them for a Hunt Ball.

''Tis a known fact,' said Mc Hi Ho, 'that Indians don't like Hunt Balls.'

'That's OK,' said Tonto, 'as long as they don't hunt mine.' The moon came out as did all the workers at the Rover car plant.

'I wonder what the folks back home are doing?' thought McGonagall. They were doing the NatWest bank in Dundee. They reached the railway crossing. Lying by the track was the train guard. 'Oh dear,' he said, 'I've just fallen off the nine-twenty from Slough. I must have nodded off. My top hat was in the guard's van keeping handy in case a Royal Person gets on.'

'Oh yes,' said McGonagall, 'most of the Royals are getting on.'

'For a start, the Queen looks eighty. It's all that sitting on the throne that does it,' said the guard. 'Do you mind if I blow my whistle?' he added, 'I like to keep in practice.' He gave a loud blast. McGonagall's horse bolted, leaving the Stoned Ranger.

'Now look what you've done,' said McGonagall. So the guard looked at what he'd done.

'I'm sorry,' said the guard, continuing to blow his whistle. 'You see, I was brought up by the Jesuits and brought down by Milly Thrills of Scunthorpe, who used appliances on me.'

'Oh, is she still around then?' said McGonagall.

'Yes, she's around eighteen stone,' said the guard. 'Look,' he said, and showed McGonagall the marks on his knee.

'What was she doing down there?' said McGonagall.

'She was a dwarf,' said the guard.

'Suddenly, during the rhumba, something got into her.'

'What was it?' said McGonagall.

'One of Dr Carter's little liver pills.'

'Och,' said McGonagall, 'so she had a little liver.'

'Yes, in Bradford she was known for it,' said the guard. 'Well, that's where *I* got to know about it.'

44

'White man's horse comes back shagged out,' said Tonto with his ear to the ground.

'Remember me?' said Dr Watson, tall in the saddle but low on money.

'Oh, it's you,' said Hi Ho McGonagall.

'You don't seem very pleased to see me,' said Watson.

'I'm as pleased as punch,' said McGonagall and punched him.

'Hello Mum,' said a big black dog.

'There must be some mistake,' said McGonagall, 'that dog thinks that I'm its mother.'

'I know,' said Watson. 'He's got very bad eyes.'

'Where's he from?' said McGonagall throwing him a tin of Wuff.

'I picked him up in Lewisham,' said Watson.

'Well, you can put him down now,' said McGonagall.

'Hello Mum,' said the dog and seized the guard's leg.

'What about this dog on my leg?' said the guard.

'Oh, he'll soon get tired of that,' said Watson.

'Well, I'm tired of it already,' said the guard. Chief Higher Water rode up with a big black dog. The Chief said, 'My dog is looking for mother.'

'Hello Mum,' said Watson's dog, dropping the railway guard.

'Me come,' said the Chief, 'to buy buffalo hide. Where your buffalo hide?'

'He hide behind tree,' said McGonagall.

'Ah,' said Watson. 'You come with pipe of peace?'

'No,' said the Chief. 'Me come with piece of pipe. Me in plumbing trade.'

'Good,' said Watson. 'Will you unblock this horse?'

'Has white man tried sink plunger?' said the Chief.

'Yes,' said the doctor.

'It's inside him.' At which moment the horse fired it.

Climbing a tree for safety the guard blew his whistle. 'Here,' he said. 'There's a buffalo hiding behind this tree.'

'Ssh, that's my dog's dinner,' said Watson.

There was a loud knocking from a wayside rosewood cupboard. McGonagall drew his gun. 'We know you're in there,' he said.

'So do I,' said a voice from inside, 'and I know you're out there.'

'So do I,' said McGonagall. 'Come out with your hands up.' He added, 'and legs down.'

'I can't,' said the voice. 'I'm a cripple.' The door opened and out stepped Quasimodo.

'What were you doing in there?' said Dr Shag Watson.

'I wasn't doing anything in there,' said Quasimodo. 'There wasn't enough room.'

'You're a very long way from Notre Dame,' said Hi Ho McGonagall.

'So are you,' said Quasi.

'Has anyone seen my Esmeralda?' said Quasi.

'No,' said McGonagall. 'Has anyone seen mine?'

DUNDEE 1850, CELTIC 3, RANGERS 0

McGonagall sat in his crofter's hut. Sometimes he stood in his crofter's hut, which is sitting down higher up. Sometimes he lay down, which is standing up in a horizontal position. He poked the fire which was the only poke he'd had all year. McGonagall wore a velvet jacket and aw', stockings, McGonagall tartan and aw', silver buckles and aw', with shoes on and a fine bonnie tam o' shanter with a cock pheasant's feather on the top and aw'.

'How do I look, Mither?' he said, and she told him. 'Naughty.' His mother set before him a jolly Scotch broth of oatmeal and thistles and aw'. 'Here,' she said. 'This will warm ye up,' and threw a red hot coal up his kilt.

The house was filled with the smell of burning hairs.

'Oh, if only your grandfather were alive to see this,' she said to the hopping figure.

'Och, Mother, you and your old Scottish jokes,' he said, beating out the flames.

'You don't know it,' she said, 'but you're one of your

47

father's old Scottish jokes. It took me an hour to get him off and aw'.'

'Och, Mother,' he said. 'I'm going to walk to Balmoral Castle.'

'You mean bugger,' said his mother. 'It's only a penny on the bus.'

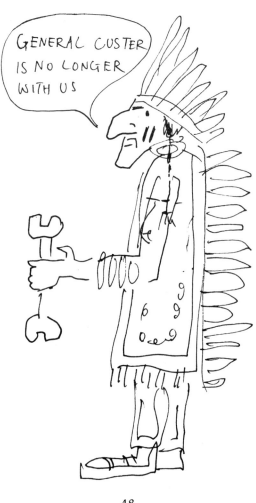

'Och, true, Mither, but there's an old Scottish saying, "The mair the mickle nicht the grinnie,"' said McGonagall.

'Yes,' said his mither. 'There's nae need for *you* to mair the mickle or nicht the grinnie. Look what it did to your father.'

Just then his father came in and McGonagall saw what it had done to him. Mind you, he looked, dear reader, like any man who had been mairing the mickle and nichting the grinnie, except his right hand wore an anti-onanist glove that dragged on the flae.

'Don't talk to me,' said Father, 'about mairing the mickle.' So no one talked to him about it.

'Have you had a hard day at the office?' said Mither to Fither.

'No,' said the blackened figure. 'I work down a coalmine.'

'Oh,' she said. 'And all these years I thought you were practising the Black Arts.'

'Oh,' said Father swallowing a live haggis. He cocked an ear.

'The pipes, the pipes,' he said in ecstasy.

'Don't worry,' said Mither. 'The plumber's coming in the morning.'

No one was more surprised than she when a Red Indian arrived at the door, with the news that Custer was dead. McGonagall swallowed the last of his thistles.

'Nay more, Mither,' he said, writhing on the flae.

'I'm proud of my wee laddie,' said the father folding his free arm.

'Och,' he moaned. 'If only I hadn't maired my mickle.'

McGonagall watched fascinated as his father crossed his third leg. 'Ach, that'll come in handy at the footba' game tomorrow,' said his father.

'I'm off,' said McGonagall.

'I know,' said his father. 'Somebody open a window.' McGonagall started to poem a song.

49

McGonagall's mother   McGonagall's father

Oooh terrible sadness at having to leave home.
Along the highways of the Queen for to roam.
I'm going awa' to see her castle
And take ma poems in a parcel.
I look forward to meeting Prince Albert
Who has his initials embroidered on his nightshirt.
And when I get to the castle gate
I will ask to be Poet Laureate.

To avoid saying goodbye to his mither and fither, McGonagall climbed out of the back window. At first McGonagall was struck by the beauty of the scenery and then by lightning. Balmoral was but thirty miles away, but using a British Rail map he did it in a hundred and fifty. The first snow of winter fell and McGonagall's all shivelled up.

'Anybody in?' he shouted at the Balmoral Castle door.

'Yes, about 920 of us,' said a voice.

'Halt, who goes there?' said a sentry.

'Well, I don't,' said McGonagall. 'Some of *you* may do.'

At that moment, the main gates opened and out shot Queen Victoria.

'Is anything worn under the kilt?' asked the Queen.

'Y fronts,' said McGonagall.

'Rubbish,' said a disappointed Queen. 'Everything is in working order.'

'Ach,' said Albert. 'Would you like to act as our Gillie?'

'No,' said McGonagall. 'I'm not a very good actor. But if I stuff a pillow up my back I can do Quasimodo.'

Albert blasted away at the sky with his shotgun. 'Shouldn't there be something up there?' said McGonagall.

'Ach, I do like banging away in heather,' said Prince Albert, disturbing several couples who already were. The Queen was doing an embroidery of Prince Albert's leg as a gift to a grateful nation.

'Aye,' said McGonagall. 'May I write a poem about the Prince's leg?' The Queen nodded. McGonagall struck an heroic pose, which misplaced his truss, which fell to the ground with a clang!

> What a wondrous sight is Prince Albert's legs,
> Hanging out from his kilt like two pegs.
> God has been very good and gives him two
> The same amount as me and you,
> But these legs are the legs of a Royal.
> Unlike you and I they don't have to toil.
> Ever since the royal marriage
> His legs have gone by carriage.
> Yes he is our good Queen's consort
> So his legs are of the best sort.
> Truly his legs are great to see
> A sign of Imperial Majesty.

'Your Maj,' said Watson. 'Are his legs insured?'

'I command you,' said the Queen, 'to journey to London and insure my husband's legs.'

In London, at the very sight of McGonagall, they rang the Lutine Bell. Watson and he were shown into Sir Terence Things.

'How's things?' said Watson.

'Ah yes, we can insure Prince Albert's legs but they'd have to be registered as an oil tanker. Now excuse me.' Sir Terence uncased a trombone. 'I play this on doctor's orders – you see, I suffer from the thrits.'

'What are the thrits?' said McGonagall.

'It's the shits spelt with a thr. What more do you want to know?'

'What's the cure?' said McGonagall.

'This is,' said Sir Things, playing a blast of 'God Save the Queen'.

'Does it keep the shits away?' said Watson.

'Yes, most of them,' said Sir Things.

McGonagall and Watson had gone to the working men's café, Woolwich, as waiters. In fact, they had been waiting to be served for an hour. McGonagall and Watson thumped the table, bouncing the HP and Daddy's sauce across to another diner. 'Ta,' he said. A black waiter came across. 'Sorry,' he said. 'We're running a little behind.'

'That's nothing,' said McGonagall, 'I've been running a little behind all my life. I use it for sitting on, what's your excuse?'

'Wot you want to eat?' said the waiter scratching them.

'After that, we'll just have a cup of tea,' said McGonagall.

'We don't serve tea to Afghans,' said the waiter.

'I'm not an Afghan, I'm a Scot,' said McGonagall.

'We don't serve dem either,' said the waiter, wiping it on his sleeve. 'We only serve Jamaicans.'

Cunningly, McGonagall said, 'My friend is Jamaican.' The waiter stared at Watson.

'But he am white,' he said, scratching them.

'Yes,' said McGonagall. 'That's fear.' In came the owner, eighteen-stone Mrs Wretch. 'What's all this?' she said.

'Well, most of it appears to be you,' said McGonagall.

'Well,' said Eighteen Stone. 'I was in the kitchen and I heard racial tension.' McGonagall rose and gave a low bow.

'Ma'am, you must be mistaken, there's no racial tension. It's just that I wear tight underpants with a feather in.'

'Oh?' said Eighteen Stone. 'I don't like the sound of that.'

So McGonagall turned the sound down.

'Is that better?' he said with a wink. 'Now, what's on the menu?'

'At the moment,' said de Jamaican, 'dere's a frying pan on it.'

'What do you recommend?' said Watson.

'I recommend another restaurant,' said Eighteen Stone. 'I want you to leave.' But they didn't leave anything. Unseen, McGonagall pocketed the cutlery.

'I want a tip,' said the waiter.

'Oh, there's a good tip at the old quarry,' said Watson and McGonagall.

In the street they collided with a Catholic priest, knocking him to the ground. Rising, he said, 'Say three Hail Marys.'

'I thought there was only one,' said McGonagall. 'She got sisters? Look Father, we know this is a poor parish, why else would you walk around in your underclothes?' The priest explained his stuff was in a machine at the Laundromat and he was walking around to get warm.

'Ah Father,' said McGonagall. 'Here's something to go with your dinner tonight,' and gave him the cutlery.

'May the Lord go with you,' said the priest.

'Yes,' said McGonagall, 'if he wants to come, it's fine by us.'

'Yes,' said Watson. 'Where is he?' The priest smiled and said, 'You ignorant bastards.' A cry of 'That's the man' came from eighteen-stone Mrs Wretch. McGonagall and Watson stood in silence as the police took the protesting priest and his cutlery away for all the unsolved murders on Scotland Yard's books. Watson, the only one with a conscience, said 'You let them arrest the wrong man.'

As they walked, an old London street cry rent the air, 'Stop thief!' Watson and McGonagall set off at speed only to be passed by the thief, then the police, then the priest with the cutlery, who paused gasping for breath and said, 'Here's something to go with your dinner,' and gave them the cutlery.

'Stop thief,' he said as Watson and McGonagall ran away. Stopping at Solly Cohen's pawn shop, Watson unveiled the cutlery from a dirty handkerchief. 'What will you give us?' said McGonagall.

'I'll give you three minutes to get out,' said Cohen, 'I'm missing *Neighbours*,' he said, disappearing into the back.

'Och,' said McGonagall, 'with him around, who wants neighbours?'

Watson winced. 'Look, McGon, *Neighbours* is an Australian soap.'

'I'm perfectly satisfied with Lifebuoy,' said McGonagall, who *knew Neighbours* was a TV series but he wanted to get a little joke in and so he did.

'Ha, ha, ha,' said Watson, who saw it coming.

'You still 'ere,' said Cohen, coming back.

'So are you,' said McGonagall.

'Look, you'll get this shop a bad name,' said Cohen.

'OK,' said McGonagall. 'How about Schmuck Macfingelstein and Sons?'

Cohen produced a pistol. 'Look, this pistol is loaded, which is more than I am.'

In desperation McGonagall said, 'Look, Mr Cohen, supposing we showed you the Star of India?'

'Can't stand him,' said McCohen. 'I seen him on the telly and he's bloody awful.' A Pakistani came in, Watson and McGonagall hid behind each other. A 'Mr Mehta' wanted to pawn his curry.

'Sorry,' said Solly, 'it's too hot for me to handle.' 'Mr Mehta' was furious. 'If you do not take my curry, I vill report you and your chicken soup to the Racing Relations Board.' 'Mr Mehta' sneezed and exploded at the back. He shouted 'Surrender', put his hands up and backed out of the room.

When the air had cleared and Cohen had regained consciousness, McGonagall spoke.

'Didn't you recognise him?'

'I didn't have time to,' said Cohen.

'Why,' said McGon. 'That was Thumby Bobagee, the Star of India.'

Watson laughed. 'He must be having a hard time,' he said. 'He certainly gave us one.'

'One?' said McGonagall. 'He let go three.' Waiting outside was the manager of the YMCA.

'This dinner bill is fading with the light, and I can't remember how much it was for.'

'That's nae a bill,' said McGonagall with a Scottish twang. 'That's a photo of Harry Secombe.'

'I still want it paid,' said the manager.

'No,' said Watson lighting his shag. 'We never had Harry Secombe, we had egg and chips.' The YMCA manager was baffled, boffled and biffled. 'Why are you doing this to me?' he said, taking snuff.

'It's the way it's written,' said Watson. 'But here's something to be going on with.'

'What is it?' said the manager.

'I don't know,' said Watson. 'It was dark when I trod on it.' It was all too much for the manager.

'Would you like a pinch of snuff?' said the manager.

'Why not?' said Watson. 'We've pinched everything else.' Two hundred sneezes later Watson started to talk to them again.

'Oh God,' said Watson. 'What went in it?'

'You did,' said McGonagall. Cohen came out.

'Look you two, you're skint, yes?' Yes they were.

'There's an amateur talent contest tonight at the Marquis of Granby.'

'Where is it?' said Watson.

'Look,' said Cohen. 'I'm a pawnbroker, not a policeman. Do you know New Cross?'

'No,' said McGonagall.

'Well that's where it is,' said Cohen. 'Look, don't go, I've had second thoughts, I'll give you something for the cutlery.'

He came back with some silver polish.
'Just my little joke,' he said.
'Just my little boot,' said McGonagall.

THE BURMESE MANGLING SERVICE

The stage was set at the Marquis of Granby. The first act was a thin juggler with three balls. He wore tights so it looked as if he had more. Then came McGonagall.

'Ladies and gentlemen, *The Charge of the Light Brigade*. Oh bravely they rode and well.' The first egg hit him on the forehead, then two more, plus tomatoes. By the time the Light Brigade had finished the charge McGonagall was covered in it, but he won the contest. The prize was a Burmese mangle. 'Och, this is great. I'll open a Burmese mangling service,' he said.

'Roll up, roll up, roll up,' said Dr Watson wearing a turban. 'Come and see the mystic Indian priest put your goods through his magic Burmese mangle.' He pointed to McGonagall now covered in brown boot polish, a crowd of curious onlookers gathered around. 'Anything put through this mangle will have magic properties, only threepence.' People came forward with ties, scarves, gloves and even grandmothers; all went through the mangle with McGonagall saying, 'Yim, bom, balla, boo. Yim, bom, balla, boo.' By the end of the day they had got three pounds sterling, and influenza.

They tried to dine at the café but the owner said, 'No Wily Oriental Gentlemen,' so it was to the public baths for

'Roll up, roll up, see mystic Indian priest put goods through
magic Burmese mangle'

sixpence. He went in brown and came out white to the amazement of the attendant.

"Ere, all his W.O.G. come off in the barf, that's 'ow they get into the country,' he said.

A totter came by. 'Any rags, bottle or bones,' he said. The attendant gave him McGonagall. The Dick Tracy radio watch spoke. 'McGonagall, where are you?' it said.

'I'm on a rag and bone cart,' said McGonagall secretively.

'Is it a disguise?' it said.

'No,' said McGonagall secretively. 'It's a rag and bone cart.'

'What have you been doing?' it said.

'Five miles an hour,' said McGonagall secretively.

'Can't you go any faster?' said Watson.

'Yes, I can,' said McGonagall jumping off the cart and running away secretively.

Back at the office Watson could see that McGonagall was in a bad way. In fact, he was in everybody's way.

'Here, drink this,' said Watson, saying 'Drink this'. McGonagall gratefully gulped it down.

'What was it?' he said.

'It's the washing-up water, the sink is blocked,' said Watson.

'Whatever got into you?' raged McGonagall.

'Nothing,' said Watson. 'It's all got into you.'

'A joke's a joke,' said McGonagall. 'But that was going too far.'

'Oh,' said Watson. 'It didn't have to go far, it was in the sink.'

The silvery voice of a woman singing approached, and there entered the Salvation Army lass, singing 'Jesus Saves'.

'I wish I could,' said McGonagall. 'Where's he keep it?'

'I'm collecting for the poor,' she said. 'What do you do with your old clothes?'

'Wear them,' said McGonagall.

'Do you,' she trilled, 'believe in life after death?'

'No,' said McGonagall. 'I'd rather have it before.'

'Have you heard of the Kingdom of God?' she trilled.

'Not lately,' said McGonagall. 'But I hear regularly from the Inland Revenue. How about you?'

'Lots of poor people sleep in the streets in freezing weather,' she said. 'It's very dangerous.'

'I know, I tripped over some of them,' said McGonagall. Finally, this dazzling display of meanness drove the girl from the premises.

'While you were away McGonagall,' said Watson, 'I solved the case of the Speckled Band, it was Glen Miller.'

'How did it happen?' asked McGonagall.

'Someone threw shit at the fan,' said Watson.

Next morning, McGonagall was up before dawn; worse still, he was up before the beak.

'Why haven't you paid your poll tax?' asked the beak.

'I'm not Polish,' replied McGonagall.

'Fined £50,' said the magistrate.

'Och, I'll do my best to find it,' said McGonagall starting to leave.

'Not so fast,' said a constable wrenching him back.

'I wasn't going fast,' said McGonagall.

'Fined another £50 for resisting arrest,' said the magistrate.

'Time to pay,' pleaded McGonagall.

'Half past four,' said the beak.

'OK, give me three hours,' said McGonagall.

'I'll do better than that,' said the beak, and gave him six months.

IS IT CHRISTMAS AGAIN?

From out the snowbound night, Dr Watson appeared. 'I made a terrible mistake. I've just come from the workhouse where I tried to give them a Christmas pudding.'

'Is it Christmas?' asked McGonagall. Watson nodded.

'So, it's happened again. We only had one last year, perhaps this is an encore,' said McGonagall.

'Now, what are you going to get for Christmas?' asked Watson.

'For Christmas,' said McGonagall, 'I'm going to get that bastard of a magistrate.'

'Are you having any of your family for Christmas?' said the snowbound Scot.

'No,' said Dr Watson. 'We're having turkey.'

'Are you a close family?' said McShagwatson.

'No,' said McGon. 'The nearest live fifty miles away.'

'Do you see much of them?' asked Watson.

'No, I told you, they live fifty miles away. Let's go home,' said McGonagall.

'Yes,' said Watson. 'I lit a fire, it should have reached the roof by now, we'll collect the insurances in the morning.'

Next morning they visited the Prudential Insurance — a Mr Grench.

'Your house is burnt down, you say?'

'Well,' said Watson. 'We haven't said it yet but when we do that's what we'll say.' Mr Grench dipped his pen in the ink.

'Where is your house?' he said.

'It's in here,' said McGonagall, pointing to a bucket of ashes.

'It's not very big.' Watson put shag in his pipe.

'How much insurance do we get?'

'I'm sorry,' said Mr Grench. 'We don't insure buckets of ashes.' McGonagall was horrified with horror.

'That's nay a bucket of ashes,' he said pirouetting on one toe. 'That is a four-bedroomed house.' He then stood in the bucket. 'There's one room for a start.' Mr Grench wasn't interested in how to start a room.

'Look, here's a pound for good will,' he said.

'Good will?' said McGonagall. 'We don't know him, can *we* keep it?'

'We're out of house and home.'

'Good,' said Mr Grench. 'Well, now I want you out of this one.'

McGonagall fainted. Watson strained to get him into the upright, but the Scot fell back, stiff as a board. Three times

Watson did this but McGonagall stayed the same: No, dear reader, I tell a lie, he now had lumps on the back of his head. A passing friendly gypsy threw a bucket of water over Watson but McGonagall still stayed unconscious. Watson fanned him with the pound note and said 'Money'. With a cry McGonagall leapt to his feet and did a *pas de deux*. The rest of the day McGonagall spent Burmese street mangling. 'Roll up, roll up,' called Watson. In fact, everything he mangled rolled up.

A vital clue had arisen. Dick Tracy radioed in.

'There's a man playing a tuba in the British Embassy in Dublin.' Our heroes needed no second bidding. The gas balloon stood ready in the recreation grounds, Catford, four men holding the ropes. Inside the gondola was a cucumber.

'What is this for?' asked McGonagall.

'You've got to eat,' said an attendant, saluting. 'We thought of everything, we even thought of Mrs Gibbs and Harold Notts.'

'Oh, are they in the gondola?' said McGon.

'No, they're in bed,' said the attendant.

'What is your name?' said Watson.

'Well,' said the embarrassed attendant, 'I'm *Mr* Gibbs.'

'Have you not had anything from Mrs Gibbs lately?' said saddened Watson.

'No, I haven't,' said the attendant. 'It's Dick Lengths who's been getting it.'

'You must have grounds for divorce,' said Watson.

'Yes,' said the saddened attendant. 'But it's two thousand pounds an acre.'

'Well, here's some to be going on with,' said McGonagall handing him the bucket of ashes.

Inside the gondola there was a safe chained to a Rottweiler and a pussy cat. 'What's the cat for?' said McGonagall.

'It's for the Rottweiler,' said Mr Gibbs. 'Let go!' So the attendants let one go and slowly the great balloon rose.

'Shouldn't we be in that?' said Watson.

'Och, it was bad timing,' said McGonagall. 'We'll ha'ter take the Steam Packet, the last time I caught a packet I was in Cairo.'

Aboard the Steam Packet they dined at the captain's table, while the captain dined at theirs.

'Why will ye nae join us at your table?' said McWatson.

'Because I don't like flatulence,' said the captain, swallowing a boiled egg.

'We are nae flatulent,' said McGon swallowing his.

'He,' said the captain, pointing a kipper at Watson, 'is guilty.' Pointing a kipper back, McGonagall said, 'But we're British and Scots.' Then, with a nautical grin, the captain said, 'I hear everything's in working order.' McGonagall told him his hadn't worked for ten years. Laughing, the captain forced a kipper down McGonagall. McGonagall forced it up again and warned the captain, 'I dinna like it.'

'It wasn't dinner, it was breakfast,' said the captain swallowing another boiled egg. 'I used to be in submarines,' he said.

'I wish you were in one now,' said McGonagall, swallowing a porridge.

'Is this a dry ship?' said Watson.

'No,' said the captain. 'It's in the water, it's the only way it works.'

'Mine works in water as well,' said McGonagall as he swallowed a boiled egg. 'Does the ship go tae Dublin?' said the canny Scot.

'Yes,' said the captain, forcing a kipper.

'What a coincidence,' said Watson, 'so are we.'

The captain forced another kipper. 'I've been at sea all my life and,' he forced kidneys on toast, 'I'll die at sea.'

'Do you mind if we watch?' said McGonagall with a twirl

of his skirt. The captain peered out of a porthole. A good peer was one of his privileges, pushing him right out was one of the crew's.

'He'll drown out there,' said Watson.

'Yes,' said the crew.

'I'll save him,' said McGonagall, diving through the port-hole and getting stuck half way.

'Throw me a life jacket,' called the captain. Immediately, Watson took off a jacket he had had all his life and threw it, with a kipper, to the captain.

'Get me out of this porthole,' said McGonagall from outside. So, with a good heave, they pushed him out.

'Splash,' he went and, 'You lotta bastards,' he went. And 'Welcome to the Irish Sea,' said the captain, passing McGona-gall a haddock.

'I must keep my strength up,' said the Scot and swallowed it.

'Well done,' said the captain.

'No it wasn't, it was raw,' said McGonagall.

'Help is coming,' cried the crew, as they watched Watson lower a boat and row out and collapse over the oars.

'Help, I'm drowning,' said the boiled-egg captain.

'Och, mon, alive you don't need any help to drown,' said McGonagall.

But a cry of 'Sharks!' soon had them back in the boat. At dawn the Steam Packet arrived at Dublin's port.

'You looking for a taxi, sir?'

'Yes,' said Dr Watson.

'So am I,' said the man. The balloon and its gondola had landed at St Stephen's Green.

'Make way,' said McGonagall who had the combination of the safe aboard. He opened sealed orders which read TO OPEN SAFE SHOOT DOG AND TURN KNOB. Carefully McGonagall raised the pistol, in one great bite the Rott-weiler swallowed it.

'For God's sake, don't let him turn around and bark,' said Watson and his shag.

'Leave him to me,' said McGonagall. 'Here,' he said, offering the dog a tit-bit. 'Nice doggie.' The nice doggie took the tit-bit as far as McGonagall's elbow, the nice doggie coughed and fired a bullet out the back that punctured a taxi's tyre.

'Who's going to pay for this?' said the driver.

'Mrs Elsie Worms,' said Dr Watson, tapping his pipe out on the Rottweiler.

'Who's Mrs Elsie Worms?' said the Irish driver.

'She's the woman who's going to pay for it,' said Dr Watson's shag. With the Rottweiler attached to McGonagall, the heroic Scot climbed into the gondola. Waiting for him was the manager of the YMCA.

'This bill is long overdue,' he said.

'How did you get here? This gondola was empty!'

'I hid in a cupboard in Ealing,' said the manager, waving the bill. McGonagall waved the Rottweiler.

'I don't believe you,' said the Scot.

'Oh, who would you believe?' said the manager, waving the bill. Waving the Rottweiler, McGonagall crossed himself. Why not, he'd crossed everybody else.

'I would believe the Pope.' The YMCA manager turned to the Pope.

'Didn't I hide in a cupboard in Ealing, your Holiness?' The Pope nodded.

'Si, dat is true, it was – a miracle.' McGonagall paused as the Rottweiler worked its way up his arm.

'Then how did you get into the gondola . . . Pope?'

'It was – a miracle.' The Rottweiler coughed and a bullet sped past the Pope's head.

'Another miracle,' said-a the Pope. 'I must-a go now. Any questions?'

'Och yes, the noo, do ye know a Mrs Gibbs?' Sorry, no,

he didn't know her. Blast, thought McGonagall, nearly had him. The YMCA manager followed as the Pope walked to his Popemobile to bless the bill.

'God bless-a da beel,' he said. The manager looked at the total, it was still the same.

'Here, your Holiness, here's a pressy of a YMCA manager, an unpaid bill and a Rottweiler.'

'It's – a miracle,' said the Popemobile and drove off.

'Is dis youse balloon?' said a silly Irish policeman. 'You can't park it here.'

'That balloon has just been blessed by the Pope,' said McGonagall.

'Oh,' said the silly Irish policeman. 'Den dat's all right den. You can keep your balloon here until the Pope's blessing wears off, dat'll be in half an hour.'

So there they were in Dublin. They met a Molly Malone, she did them a power of good. As Dr Watson said, 'We've got to get some sleep soon or we'll forget how to.'

SIR HENRY
HEARS THE BELLS

Back in London, our heroes hurried hurriedly to the office.

'You're back,' said Miss Moneypenny.

'You're front,' said McGonagall and embraced it.

'Since you've been away, guess what I've learnt?' she said, inflating her bosom.

'Let me guess?' said McGonagall. 'You've learnt Yugoslavian,' he said.

'That's one,' she said.

'You've learnt one Yugoslavian?' he said, bending down and looking at her through his legs. The telephone went. All three listened intently to the bell, it was great fun and harmless.

A great actor in a fur coat climbed in through the window, it was Sir Henry Irving.

'The bells,' he acted. 'I hear the bells.' Slowly, he approached the telephone on tiptoe. 'The bells, the bells,' he repeated. Then striking a pose and holding Watson by the seat of his trousers, he said, 'Answer that fucking phone.' Watson eased himself free but lost a few hairs.

'It would kill the spell to answer it,' he said.

'Fuck the spell,' said Sir Henry, picking up the phone.

'Hello,' he said. He handed the phone to McGonagall, 'It's for you. It's your mother.'

'Hello Mither,' he said with a wave. 'I've told you never to ring me at the butcher's.' The phone rang again.

'The bells,' said Sir Henry, striking a striking pose. He picked up the handset. 'Yes?' he snapped.

'This is the butcher,' said a voice.

'This is the actor,' said Sir Henry. 'Have you any kidneys?'

'Course I have,' said the butcher. 'Everyone's got 'em.'

'Yes,' said the actor. 'Have you any sausages?'

'No, I've run out of 'em.'

'So have I, what a coincidence,' said the actor, who then lowered his trousers to his ankles. Miss Moneypenny screamed.

'Don't worry, me dear,' said Sir Henry. 'I'm just airing my legs, they suffer with claustrophobia.' All watched, fascinated by the great actor's legs. Suddenly he clenched his knees up and down.

'Does that hurt?' said Watson.

'No,' said the actor.

'OK, well does that hurt?' he said throwing a rock at them.

'Yes, that hurt,' said the great actor, who started to pull his trousers up. Miss Moneypenny screamed as they disappeared. The office door opened, there stood the butcher.

'I managed to find some sausages,' he said, opening his parcel.

'So did I,' said the actor, opening his. It was the end of an interesting day.

They had an urgent call from the zoo.

'We got trouble with our elephant,' said the keeper.

'We'll be round as soon as we've cooked these sausages,' said Dr Watson.

It was an unusual case. Somehow or other a man had got inside the elephant.

'How do you know he's in there?' said Watson.

'I can hear him singing.'

'Hello,' said McGonagall, tapping on the elephant. 'Who's that in there?'

'Tom Corbett,' came the answer.

'How did you get in there?' said McGonagall.

'It's loss of memory,' said Corbett. 'And can I borrow a lawnmower, the grass in here is a foot tall and I can't see.'

'This is our best elephant, you must come out,' said the keeper.

'No,' said Corbett. 'I need the publicity.'

'Leave this to me,' said Watson. Carefully he placed an eviction order in a bun and gave it to the elephant.

'You swines,' said Corbett when he got it.

'It's a miracle,' said the Pope. 'Another case solved.'

THE HAGGIS AND THE
BOWSER, PART II

One stormy night, with the haggis falling heavily, McGonagall and Dr Watson sought shelter in a Scottish croft.

'Hae ye shelter for a night?' they cried. A suspicious
landlord shouted, 'Molly, come and look. Who'd come out
on a night like this – bring the camera.' A huge bursting
woman arrived; together they took photographs and roared
with laughter, then slammed the door. McGonagall hammered, again the door opened.

'Hae ye shelter for the night?' they cried. Again, the
couple roared with laughter. 'Who'd come out on a night
like this,' they said, and slammed the door, but not before
McGonagall and Watson had nipped in.

'What are you doing in here?' roared the crofter.

'Nothing,' said McGonagall. 'We haven't had time to.'
The hairy crofter thought, 'The Lair McReekie, *he'd* come
out on a night like this. Also, Margaret Menzies, the two
Luff brothers and Mrs McKenzie, they'd all come out on a
night like this.'

'Then why haven't they?' said McGonagall.

'Och,' said the monstrous wife taking McGonagall by the
throat and holding him up. 'Now tell the truth Jamies, what
were you two doing out on a night like this?'

'Freezing,' said McGonagall.

'You must be mad,' they said. They led them skilfully
into a bedroom full of nude Napoleons and Hitlers. They'd
come out on a night like this. A Hitler came over and hit
Watson.

'That's for Stalingrad,' he said, while Napoleon kicked McGonagall. 'That's for Waterloo.' Watson retaliated, he hit several Hitlers. 'That's for Charing Cross,' he said. McGonagall clouted half-a-dozen Napoleons. 'That's for Chicken Marengo.' By dawn they'd got all the Hitlers and Napoleons cowering in a corner to records of Des O'Connor.

'Des O'Connor must be bombed,' raged a Hitler. 'Zat goes for Ann Shelton and Vera Lynn.' Hitler sidled up to McGonagall. 'I'm zer real Hitler, all zese are phoneys.'

'Have you had breakfast?' said the crofter.

'No,' said Watson.

'Well, we've had ours,' said the crofter (Frank Carson 1909–91).

From the door came a knocking, a banging, a doorbell, a hammering, a police whistle and police siren.

'It's the Bill,' said the crofter, hiding in the porridge.

'The bill,' said McGonagall from under a floorboard. 'I thought these lodgings were free?'

'So did I,' said Watson, hiding behind the nude Hitlers. A Scots policeman wearing a kilt entered. He walked around the back of the nude Hitlers and spoke to Watson.

'Ah sir, you must be the one with the suit, a man of substance.'

'I have nothing to hide, officer,' he said, so the policeman gave him a walnut.

'You can hide this, sir. Any convenient orifice will do.'

With the policeman watching, Dr Watson inserted it into one of the nude Hitlers. The Scots policeman took out a notebook.

'Now, is the owner in?'

'What is the nature of your enquiry?' said McGonagall rising from under his floorboard and throwing the policeman off.

'What are yew doing down there, sir?'

70

'I'm getting up,' said McGonagall (Frank Carson 1909–91).

'Pliss hurry up,' said the nude Hitlers. 'Ve are getting cold.'

'Och, officer,' said the hairy crofter, rising out of the porridge, 'I could nae hold my breath any longer, I know why ye are here.'

'So do I,' said the policeman. 'We believe that this establishment is being run as a bawdy house by Cynthia Payne, using under-aged Hitlers and Napoleons. Now are you going to come quietly or shall I use the ghetto-blaster?' The hairy crofter rose further out of the cauldron.

'But can't you see I'm already doing porridge?' The Scottish policeman was stunned. He took off his helmet and scratched his head. 'Och, it's Mair the Mickle,' he said, replacing his helmet. It was plain to see it was back to front but it showed there was a new sense of adventure abroad in the Scottish police.

'Where is the mistress of the house?' said the Scot of a policeman.

'She's out having a shag, will the wife do?' said the porridge-clad crofter. The constable of Old Scotland sneezed and his wig fell off, it was seized by the cat who set off with his prize.

'Yes, your wife will do, she'll do six months.'

'What is the charge? My wife is innocent. Why, she hasn't even seen mine.'

'Be careful what you say,' said the policeman. 'We have the negatives.'

'That pussy cat has stolen my wig,' said the policeman. 'The cost of replacement is £8.' The crofter was now clear of the porridge and was dripping it on McGonagall lying on the floor. He could see right up the crofter's kilt.

'Och,' said McGonagall. 'No wonder your wife won't leave.' I know a Mrs Gibbs who would be glad of that.'

'Now, now,' said the police. 'That's enough of that.'

'Constable, she's never had enough of that,' said McGonagall rising from the flae. 'And while I'm up, have you a search warrant?'

'Nay, I have no search warrant, but in the boot of my car I have a date pudding.'

'I have a whale's tooth sewn into my sporran,' said McGonagall.

The porridge-caked crofter shouted, 'My grandfather has a drainpipe down his trousers for the run off.'

The hairy crofter's huge wife appeared carrying a wig. 'What a bit of luck,' she said. 'I have just found this in the cat's box. It fits fine, I'll use it as a Bowser*.'

'Can ve haff zer heating up,' said the nude Hitlers.

'Up where?' said the crofter.

'Up yours,' said the Hitlers. Boom boom boom from outside came the beating of a bass drum. He was a thin bandsman wearing spectacles. He marched around the room swinging his drumsticks and caused havoc as he marched through the nude Hitlers. For good effect the crofter picked him up and stood him in the porridge. Pinning his arms to his sides the policeman said, 'We can't hear what you're saying.' The drummer said he was lost.

'Have ye nae seena pipe band go past here, for aw I knae they might be playing a different tune by now.' Swinging his drumsticks he counter marched through the middle of the Napoleons.

'Quelle flummox,' they said. At that moment, the drum skin burst and out spilled Quasimodo.

'It's a miracle,' said the Pope.

'You're a long way from France, Quasi,' said Dr Watson.

'Aye, he's a long way from the ceiling as well.'

---

* Wig for a bald fanny.

72

'Has anyone seen my Esmeralda?' said the dwarf.

'No,' said the policeman, 'has anyone seen mine?'

'Yes,' said the crofter. 'I seen her, she's bloody ugly.'

Down the chimney came a choking cloud of soot. A blackened figure crashed into the porridge.

'Ho, ho, ho, a Merry Christmas,' said the figure.

'Och, it's Father Christmas.'

Boom, boom, boom went the drummer.

'It's no good,' said Quasimodo, 'I can't stay in this drum any longer.'

'You'll never be any bloody longer,' said McGonagall.

'My beautiful Esmeralda, I wonder what she is doing now?'

At that moment she was trying to get the stains out.

'It's a miracle,' said the Pope.

'Now it's time for presents,' said Father Ho Ho. 'For the crofter's wife I have . . . a Bowser.'

'I've already got one,' she said.

'Oh dear,' said Father Christmas. 'The time I took shaving it off the cat.'

'Does anyone want a tune?' said the thin drummer.

'Aye,' said the porridge crofter. 'Do you know Kettelby's "Bells Across the Meadow"?'

'Yes.'

'Well bring it in, it's getting rusty.' Off went the boom boom boom after the bell.

'Now,' said the huge crofter's wife. 'Who would like a drop of the hard stuff?'

'I all would,' they said. She gave them each a piece of concrete. It was a humble crofter's wife's joke.

'Ooohh,' said Quasimodo, playing with his lump of concrete. 'I must get back to my Esmeralda and ring the bell.' An ambulance pulled up outside. A man came in, it was St John.

'Anyone had an accident?' he asked hopefully. 'I've got a stretcher in the ambulance.'

'Good,' said McGonagall. 'Stretch him,' he pointed at Quasimodo.

OCH, THE NOO I

The Dick Tracy watch activated.

'Hello, McGonagall?'

'Hello, Dick?'

'Yes, it's Dick, where are you?' said Tracy.

'I'm in the middle of some nude Hitlers.'

'Of course you are. Now listen, can the nude Hitlers hear what I'm saying?'

'No,' said McGonagall.

'The man who knows about the missing Prime Minister is working with Billy Cottle's Circus and Zoo. You must inveigle your way in.'

Our heroes went straight to the circus to do an inveigle.

'Och, the noo,' said McGonagall in Celtic tones. 'I knae how to get in.' Watson pulled on his pipe, it was that Condor feeling. After a good feel he finally said 'How?' McGonagall tapped his nose, waggled his eyebrows and gave a cunning wink, silly sod. 'We just ha tae buy tae tickets.' At the box office he repeated his secret method of entering the big top.

'Tae seats,' he said.

'What the fuck do you mean, tae?' said the ticket man.

'My friend,' said Watson to the ticket man, 'has a speech impediment.'

'Oh,' said the ticket man, 'then why is he clutching his arse?'

'The problem is deep rooted,' said Watson. 'We would like two tickets tae the show.'

'That will be five pounds.' Both our heroes fainted. A passing gypsy threw a bucket of water over them etc.

'Hoi Hup La,' said McGonagall leaping to his feet. 'I dinna ken there were showers here.' Watson made a thirty-yard run and arrived at the box office.

'Look I'm new here,' he said. 'How much are tickets?'

'Six pounds,' said the ticket man.

'Good God,' said shag Watson. 'A moment ago they were five pounds.'

'Yes,' said the ticket man, 'that's inflation for you.'

'How much for my friend here who is under fourteen?'

The ticket man gave a rude guffaw. 'Under fourteen? He looks old enough to be under six foot.'

Watson gave a cough that came out the other end.

'My friend looks old because he is on steroids.' The ruse worked. McGonagall got in half price but had to hold Watson's hand all the way through. Once inside, they found their way to their seats; so there was nothing clever in that, lots of people were finding their way to their seats, it was perfectly normal, any reader will know how easy it is, once you have bought your tickets, to find your seats. Well, so it was with Watson and McGonagall, they found no difficulty going to their seats, all you had to do was to tally the number on your tickets with the numbers on the backs of seats. McGonagall's and Watson's were J13 and J14, so it was unexplainable as to why they were in K12 and K11, and it would appear it wasn't that easy for them after all, especially as they held hands all through the show. The Dick Tracy watch activated.

'McGonagall? We think the man is appearing as a gorilla.'

Thank God, thought Watson, that they had brought the gorilla skin, just in case. Round the back of the tent McGonagall got into the gorilla suit. It took a few moments for Watson to let him into the cage with the other gorillas, and it was but a few moments before McGonagall was rendered senseless. While the gorilla keeper was getting McGonagall out, Dr Watson threw a bucket of water over a passing gypsy.

'God bless, you, sir,' said the soaking figure. Any other gypsy would have said, 'Ho hoi hup la, I didn't know there were showers in here.' Mind you, he did smash his violin over Watson's head.

'Och,' said McGonagall, 'that gorilla is in a skin but it's his ain.' It was early closing in Lewisham.

A clown drew nigh. 'I juggle with balls,' he said.

'Well,' said Watson, 'you're not going to juggle with mine.'

'Roll up, roll up,' shouted the ringmaster. 'Any volunteers to be fired from the cannon — a hundred-pound prize?'

'Did you hear that?' said Watson excitedly, running after McGonagall and stuffing him down the barrel.

'Fire!' shouted the cannoneers. There was a scream as a bundle shot out the cannon into the bandstand.

'Are you all right up there?' said Watson.

'I'm nae up there, I'm still in the cannon, those were my clothes.' In one bound Watson had McGonagall out and dressed.

'Where's the hundred pounds?' he said.

'We didn't get it, you didn't go,' said Watson fuming. 'You stayed in the barrel you little fool.' Struggling and shouting McGonagall was stuffed down the barrel again.

'It's your turn in the barrel,' shouted McGonagall.

'Fire!' shouted the cannoneer. A loud bang, the figure of the screaming McGonagall flew up into the gallery.

'Look,' said Watson counting and recounting. 'A hundred

pounds,' he said to the charred smoke-blackened figure. A passing gypsy, with a shower fitting, passed by.

'That was a terrible thing tae do to me,' wailed the smoking McGonagall.

The beautiful bare-back lady passed by.

'Oh! Poor little thing,' said Watson.

'Can you see it then?' said McGonagall.

'That shot from the cannon was the bravest I've seen,' she said. 'Come to my caravan and I'll soothe the lumps.' The caravan shook as she soothed the helpless Scot. The crowd could hear his plaintive cry of 'Nae mair lassie, nae mair', his voice getting weaker and weaker. Finally, what looked like a bundle of old clothes was thrown out the caravan door. Somewhere, in there, was McGonagall. Watson put a raffle ticket on it and tried to sell him.

'I'll have nae mair of this,' said McGonagall tearing up the sign 'For Sale, Tiger Meat'. Then he poemed,

> Oooohhh terrible experience in the gorilla cage,
> I'll never do that again I'll wage.
> As for being used as a cannon ball,
> I didn't like that at all.
> And being sold as tiger meat,
> Was not my idea of a treat.

In search of their quarry our heroes searched the circus.

'You won't find a quarry in 'ere,' said a big security guard.

'Are you a security guard?' said McGonagall.

'Yes,' said the man.

'Well, we're very dissatisfied with you, we both feel very insecure.'

'Come and sit by the elephants,' he said. 'You'll feel better. People who sit near elephants always feel more secure.' So they both sat by the elephants.

'It's not working,' said McGonagall. 'This elephant keeps searching our pockets, he's had all the sandwiches out of my sporran.' The security man burst into tears.

'I'm sorry,' he said, 'that's Harold, he's the elephant that keeps letting me down. You are a naughty elephant,' he said, wiping away tears and tying a knot in his trunk.

'These sandwiches taste lovely,' said a voice inside the elephant. It was Corbett.

'Yes, he's been in there a week,' said the security man. 'He comes and goes, it depends when the elephant's had enough.'

Could this security man know of a man in a gorilla skin?

'Yes, ha ha,' said the security man. 'Just a little while ago, a bloke got in a gorilla suit and the real gorilla beat the shit out of him.'

'That man was me,' said McGonagall.

'Oh, ha ha,' went on the security man.

'Remind me,' said McGonagall 'to buy you a crumbling cliff for your birthday.'

'Quick,' said the ringmaster. 'Ladies and gentlemen, the gorilla has escaped and is now appearing on the moors.' All gave chase.

'There he is, up that tree!' went up the cry.

'Shake the tree with the elephant,' went up the cry. With a howl, the gorilla crashed down through the hundred-foot tree at the feet of our heroes.

'Now to get my own back!' cried McGonagall, jumping up and down on the helpless creature's head.

'For Christ's sake, somebody stop him!' cried the gorilla.

'A talking gorilla,' said the ringmaster. 'He's worth a fortune.'

'Oh,' said McGonagall. 'Where does he keep it?'

'There's a man in the gorilla.' The security man put his ear to its stomach.

'Is that you, Corbett? You do get about.'

'Let me out,' said the writhing gorilla.

'That voice,' said Watson. 'It's Joan Sutherland, let her out.'

Carefully they unzipped the gorilla skin with screams as they caught the short and curlies, and out spilled James Bond wearing jockey pants.

'You impostor!' shouted an outraged William McGonagall. 'You're not Joan Sutherland, you're someone else.'

'Everyone back to the circus,' went up the cry.

'A moment sur,' said a yokel with a stick that went up the cry. 'We 'eard a animal was loose on the moors, is it a hoax?'

'No,' said McGonagall. 'It was a gorilla.'

'A gorilla? And there was me looking for a hoax.'

'That skin be empty zur,' went up his cry.

'You just gobbed on my boot,' said Watson.

'Did I, zur? Thanks for tellin' me, I got a very bad memory for things.'

'Well you try and remember this,' said Watson gobbing on the yokel's boot.

A band marched by all out of step, their leader shouted 'Halt'. Gradually the band stopped in a scrunched up bunch.

''Ave you see a bass drummer? We lost 'im in the Highlands, and we bin out of step ever since.'

In the circumstances it was the last thing the leader and his band needed, but Watson, after a demonstration, sold him the gorilla skin. Mind you it took three hours of McGonagall having to climb several trees in the skin. It was a fine sight as the out-of-step band marched away with a gorilla at the head.

'Sorry about gobbin' on your boot,' said the yokel. 'My eyes aren't what they used to be, they used to be my ears.'

'You know,' said Watson as he read the evening paper. 'We should never have sold that band leader the gorilla skin, someone's shot him.'

The circus was very busy, the dwarves were on, so were the clowns and the highwire walker. McGonagall searched everywhere for the man in the gorilla suit.

'There's nae sign of him,' he said.

'It's unlikely a man in a gorilla suit would go around signing things,' said Watson. 'Who's to say that the man,' said Watson filling his pipe with shag, 'is not disguised as an admiral in the Argentine Navy?'

'I could say it,' said McGonagall.

Filling his pipe with more shag, Watson said, 'I bet you five pounds you can't stand on the elephant and say it.' McGonagall took a pace back and fell off the elephant.

'Look,' said the security guard. 'You're worrying the elephant, he's not supposed to carry Scotsmen with everything under the kilt in working order, you'll have to get off, kneel . . . no, I didn't mean you, I meant the elephant.' The elephant is not known for its eyesight. Neither is McGonagall and that is why an elephant was kneeling on him. Using three-in-one oil they eased him out.

'You've got oil on my elephant's knees,' grumbled the security man. 'He'll never win a prize like that.'

'It'll stop his knees squeaking,' said McGonagall.

Watson passed McGonagall a five-pound note.

'That's all I've got,' he said.

'Now it's all I've got,' said McGonagall. 'What was that all about?'

'It's about five pounds,' said Watson.

'You were right,' said the security man, 'his knees *have* stopped squeaking.' The lovely bare-back rider came by on a white horse. McGonagall hid behind the elephant.

'Have you seen much of the Scotsman?' she said.

'No, I think you saw more of him than anybody,' said Watson.

'Why are you hiding behind that elephant,' said the security man.

'I wasn't hiding,' said McGonagall. 'I was listening to his knees.'

'Would you like to buy an elephant?' said the security man.

'An elephant, ha ha ha,' said Watson. 'What would I do with an elephant?'

'You could oil his knees,' said the security man.

'No, no, no,' said McGonagall. 'My elephant dog would kill him.'

'Oh?' said the security man. 'How can a dog kill an elephant?'

'He waits,' said McGonagall.

'An elephant never forgets,' said the security man.

'Well, you can forget this one for a start,' said Watson.

'Will you stop all that noise out there,' said a voice from inside the elephant. 'There's people in here trying to sleep.'

There was the wailing of police sirens, the flying squad car sent the security man flying. Out dashed several policemen with pistols, using a loud hailer they shouted at the elephant.

'We know you're in there, Corbett, come out with your hands up and your legs down.'

'Come and get me,' snarled Corbett.

'I'm afraid,' said a policeman, 'we must take this elephant into custody.'

The court case was delayed as they manoeuvred the elephant into the witness box.

'What is the elephant charged with?' said the Judge.

'Well, m'lud,' said a policeman. 'For a start he charged one of the policemen.'

'So he's charged with a charge,' said laughter-in-court Judge.

'What is the elephant charged with?'

82

'First witness,' said the Judge, 'and silence in court.'

'Name?'

'William Topaz McGonagall,' said William Topaz McGonagall.

'Tell the court in your own words what happened,' said the silence-in-court.

'Very well,' said McGonagall. 'Tharlux fricklesplun twottick.'

'What are those?' said the mystified Judge.

'These are some of my own words . . .' began McGonagall.

'Wheeeeeeeeeeeeeooooouuuuuughhhhh,' went the elephant from one end.

'Control that elephant, sergeant.'

The solicitor for the defence, Terence Nistule, donned his pyjamas and climbed into a sleeping-bag. 'The defence rests,' he said.

'Now, Mister McGonagall,' said the Judge, 'continue with your evidence.'

'Silence in court!' shouted McGonagall.

'M'lud,' said shag Dr Watson. 'My friend William Topaz McGonagall is the victim of a broken marriage.' So saying he emptied a load of rubbish from a sack.

'What are these?' he said.

'These are the pieces of a broken marriage,' said Watson.

'Will the accused stand,' said the m'lud.

'I am standing,' said McGonagall. 'But there's a hole in the witness box.'

'How do you feel?' said the Judge.

'On the hole, OK,' said the Scot.

'Have you anything to say before I pass sentence?' said the Judge.

'Yes, I say that if you go down in the woods today be sure of a big surprise.'

'Anything else?' said the Judge.

McGonagall and Watson clearing the court

'Yes sir, today's the day the teddy bears have their picnic.'

'Silence in court and Lewisham,' said the m'lud. 'I remand you all except the elephant for a doctor's report.' At once Dr Watson fired a pistol.

'That's my report.'

'Clear the court,' said the clerk. In half an hour McGonagall and Watson had cleared the court and had it all in the back of a van.

'Och, there's nothing like driving along the king's highway,' said McGonagall.

'We aren't,' said Watson. 'We're stuck in a bloody ditch.'

'Din nae worry,' said the confident Scot, 'I'll call the AA.'

As night was falling a crowd of drunks from Alcoholics Anonymous arrived and helped push the truck further in the ditch.

'HERE'S FINE BLOODY MESS YOU'VE GOT US INTO,' said Watson. An RAC patrol came by, the driver Lord Sythe-Wallington got out.

'I say you low-class pissed people, you are blocking the road and Her Majesty Queen Elizabeth is due past here any minute now.'

Lord Sythe-Wallington was a practising psychologist. 'All you drunks, listen. If you follow me, I'll take you all to McEwans Whisky distillery.' A great cheer went up.

Like sheep they followed Lord Sythe-Wallington in his RAC van and he safely led them over Beachy Head.

'Well, bai Jove, I've seen them on their way, now we'll have to get this van of yours out of the ditch – you'll have to offload,' he said. Looking into the back of the lorry, he came back staggered. 'You got an elephant in the back, what's he doing in there?'

'You'll find it on the floor.'

'Bai Jove, yes it's knee deep,' said the RAC fellow. To his horror and hirrer there was the Queen coming up the road.

'It'll take a long time for that to clear,' said Watson.

MISS MONEYPENNY AND THE
NUDE BANJO PLAYER +
A DASH FOR THE HORIZON

Our heroes returned to their office in Baker Street. Waiting for them was a Wallington Throtts, ear, nose and throat doctor and used car salesman. He said, 'I see I've arrived in the nick of time, your left ear is far too small for your right ear, that is not correct.' He took a pair of pliers from his pocket. 'See if I can give it a stretch.'

McGonagall backed off.

'Wait a minute, sir,' he said, going to hide in the cupboard, only to find a nude man inside about to play a banjo.

'Miss Moneypenny,' said Dr Watson, putting on his

glasses to improve the view, 'what is the meaning of this?'

'I know it looks bad,' she said.

'Bad?' said Watson. 'It looks huge.' Wallington Throtts was trying to stretch McGonagall's small ear and both of them were wrestling on the flae.

'I dinna want my ear any bigger,' shouted the Scot.

'You silly man,' said Wallington Throtts. 'Unless you have matching ears, the wind will get behind the big one and spin you off your feet.'

'Any requests?' said the nude banjoist.

'Yes,' said Watson, 'get dressed and bugger off.' The nude banjoist stood up in a rage, hitting his head on the top of the cupboard and crashing unconscious to the flae atop of his banjo which let out a cheery twang. McGonagall now had Wallington Throtts in an arm lock.

'All right, let me go! If it's not your ears you want seen to, what about various veins, piles or la Grippe?' The door opened and three attendants from the local asylum came in.

'Now,' said the one with the moustache. 'Which one of you is the nude banjoist?'

'Oh dear,' said Miss Moneypenny. 'You're not taking him away so soon, he's not played a tune yet.'

'Ah,' and the attendant's voice showed recognition. 'Come along, Throtts. I'm afraid, folks, this man is the noted ear stretcher from Catford. There's twenty people he's had a go at that can't go out in high winds.' The nude banjoist came to and immediately struck up 'The Stars and Stripes Forever'.

'That's funny,' said Miss Moneypenny. 'He doesn't look like an American.'

'None of them do without clothes, ma'am,' said the attendant.

'Before you take me away,' said Wallington Throtts, 'the only way you'll get your ear back to normal is to hold an omelette to it.'

'Miss Moneypenny,' said McGonagall. 'Beat up an omelette, will you.' It had been a near thing. The omelette didn't last long on McGonagall's ear, as in a fit of hunger Watson ate it, even managing to get a dash of HP sauce on it.

'Look Watson, you can't go around putting HP sauce on people's ears.'

Watson burst into tears. 'All my life I've tried to keep it a secret, I've been an HP sauce and eareater since birth, but I think the horror of your ear has finally cured me, thank you my Scottish friend and your ear.'

The men shook hands and became firm friends.

'Look, McGonagall,' said Dr Watson, who was seriously engaged in looking. 'We'll have to put the case of the missing Prime Minister on hold, it's been six months now and the six pounds fifty the Chancellor of the Exchequer gave us as a float has nearly run out.'

In a flash McGonagall had the begging bowl out. Dr Watson sang in his powerful baritone, 'Drake is going west', while McGonagall slept by his side.

'You do five till ten, and I'll do ten till two,' said Watson.

Dawn, and a lone policeman saw two sleeping figures by a bowl containing three pounds in small change. It was against the law to sleep in the street. It was also against the law to steal three pounds from a begging bowl.

'Stop!' The voices of Watson and McGonagall rang through the soft morning air. The constable halted. 'Ah, you are awake, gentlemen. I have been keeping watch over your money as you slept, there you are,' he said, handing them a pound. They returned back to the office where they counted the pound again.

It was time McGonagall went home, so he and Watson caught the train to Dundee.

'Och son,' said his mither. 'I've got thistle and chips ready for ye.'

'Never mind that, what has happened to the house?'

'Och,' said his mither. 'We left a light in the window for you. Nothing much happened except the hoose burnt doon.'

'Never mind that, where are the rest of the family?'

'Och,' said his mither. 'They all went off to join the Foreign Legion.'

So it was Watson and McGonagall for Sidi bel Abbes.

'Och,' said Mither. 'Goodbye, and if you ever find your father, ask him what he did with the fish knives.' Never mind that, he would find the family fish knives and restore them to their former glory. Now where was Sidi bel Abbes?

To find out, they attended Mrs Doris Garkle, a spiritualist. They all sat round a table in a dark room. She made Watson and McGonagall hold hands, then she went into a trance.

'Is anybody there?' she said.

'Yes, *we* are,' said Watson.

'No, no, no,' said Doris. 'Is anybody there from Sidi bel Abbes?'

'Yes, I am,' said her husband through a hole in the ceiling.

'Oooohhhhh, tell us, oh mystery one,' said Doris. 'Who is Sisi bel Abbes?'

'That's the wrong name,' said McGonagall. 'It's not Sisi, it's Sidi.'

'Ohhhhh,' groaned Doris Garkle. 'Correction, who is Sidi bel Abbes?'

'Just a moment,' said the voice in the ceiling and went to consult a dictionary.

'Ah, here we are,' said the hole in the ceiling. 'It's a foreign legion fort in Algiers and that will be a pound.'

Watson and McGonagall boarded an 11a bus.

'Two to Algiers,' they said.

'Och, we only go as far as Princes Street,' said the conductor.

Travelling thus, it took then a hundred changes of buses to get to a building that looked familiar.

'Hello son, you're back again,' said his mother. McGonagall was stunned.

'Mither dear, what are you doing in Sidi bel Abbes?'

His mother said, 'Never mind that, why are you both dressed like Foreign Legionnaires in Dundee?'

'Och,' said McGonagall. 'We got the wrong bus.' McGonagall couldn't sleep that night until he remembered you had to do it lying down. Next day, still in their Legionnaire's uniforms, they went to the French Embassy. The ambassador appeared at the door in his pyjamas.

'Sacré bleu,' he said. 'What are you men doing here? I didn't order any soldiers. I mean we are not at war, are we?'

'No, no, no, Jamie,' said McGonagall. 'We've come to join up.'

'Oh, mon Dieu,' said the ambassador. Hardly had the words left his lips, when there appeared at the door a beauteous woman in a see-through nightdress. She shook the ambassador by the throat.

'You swine of le man, you didn't finish, you left me lying on the bed.'

'Oh, it's cold standing here,' said the ambassador. 'State your business.'

'I,' said Dr Watson, 'am a doctor.'

'Well, you don't dress like one,' said the ambassador.

'You don't dress like an ambassador,' said Watson.

'Listen Jamie, we're dressed to join the Foreign Legion.'

'Do you speak French?' asked the ambassador.

'No,' said le Watson.

'Then you are no good. I mean ze sergeant will shout his ordaires in French. Le stand at ease he will say, and you won't understand.'

'Will you hurry up,' came the female screams from up-stairs.

'I'm coming, darling,' said the ambassador.

'Well don't do it down there, come up here.'

'Don't start without me,' shouted the ambassador.

'Look, I can understand le French,' said McGonagall.

'You must be the only one who does,' said le ambassador.

'Listen,' said McGonagall. 'Le stand at le ease, slope les arms, le right turn, ferme la porte.' The ambassador fermed the porte.

'He's fermed the porte,' said le Watson. Watson hammered on the door.

'Ouvre la porte,' they shouted as they hammered. Inside le ambassador hammered back.

'Le go away,' he shouted.

'Ouvre this porte,' shouted le McGonagall. 'Or we'll put something nasty through the box de letters.' There was silence from the ambassador. The door opened and a gypsy threw a bucket of water over them. The wife had now hurried down the stairs in her see-through nightdress.

'Begone, let my lover the ambassador get on with his duties. You have confused him, he doesn't know where he is.'

'Well he knows where yours is,' said Dr Watson. 'Madame, I'm willing to give you a thorough examination without payment.'

'Very well,' she said. 'Behind this screen.' Behind the screen a gypsy threw a bucket of water over him. Dripping wet and shouting, 'I'll kill that bloody gypsy,' Dr Watson gave madam a thorough examination. It went on for three days and three nights, while the ambassador and McGona-gall slept in the hall.

'Does 'ee usually take this long?' said the ambassador. Just then madam appeared pushing Dr Watson in a wheel-chair.

'I'm afraid the examination 'as taken it out of him,' she said. 'In fact, he's only just taken it out of me.'

'This is an outrage,' said the French ambassador. 'You 'ave violated French territory, we must fight a duel, name your weapons.'

'I name my weapon Ronald Coleman,' said Watson.

'Good,' said the Frenchman. 'We meet at dawn tonight at the Bois de Boulogne, I will take the night flight, darling.'

THE SCENE: DAWN, THE BOIS DE BOULOGNE

The ambassador and his seconds stood shivering in the cold morning air, while in Mrs Lunn's boarding house in Dundee Dr Watson lay warm and cosy in bed.

'Wake up, mon,' said McGonagall from his bed in the chest of drawers. 'You'll miss the duel of honour.'

Watson stirred. 'I'm not going to miss anything, he's going to miss me.'

The landlady came in with a cup of tea. 'Which one of you is table d'hôte?' she said. McGonagall pointed at the sleeping Watson.

'Oh, right,' said the landlady. 'He said 'e wanted to be wakened with a cup of tea.' She threw it on him.

'Aggggggg. Agggggggggghhhhhhhhh and Aggggggggggg-ggghhhhh again,' said Watson. 'Was that the gypsy?'

'Ye craven coward,' said McGonagall, scratching his wedding tackle. 'That poor frog ambassador is out there in the freezing bois with no one to shoot at.' Watson wrestled with his conscience and krupled his blurzon, then both men caught the night ferry cattle boat to Calais. As long as they stayed in the middle of the flock and went 'baa baa' they were safe. In the Bois de Boulogne the frog ambassador said, 'I can't wait for my opponent any longer, it's been two days and nights. I'll fire my pistol at where he should have been.' Le Bangggg! A shot rang out in the clear morning air.

'Am I too late, m'sieur?' said Watson arriving on scene.

'Oui oui,' said the ambassador.

A caped French detective drew nigh, he pointed in a direction.

'Mon dieu,' he said.

'You must be mistaken,' said McGonagall. 'I am not mon dieu, neither is my friend a mon dieu, but some of our best friends are mon dieus.'

'Are you or are you not trying to join the Foreign Legion?'

'Am I too late for the duel, m'sieur?'

'Yes,' said McGonagall. 'We are and are not trying to join the Foreign Legion.'

'Then,' said the cloaked detective, 'follow moi.' They followed moi to the recruiting depot. There they were made to strip for a medical examination.

'Ow long as it been like that?' said the frog doctor.

'That's as long as it's ever been,' said McGonagall. Both men were passed fit and ready to be killed by Arabs. A week later they arrived at the Fort Sidi bel Abbes. A Legion dance was in progress. Soon Watson and McGonagall were dancing with the rough Legionnaires.

'Do you come here often?' said a rough soldier to McGonagall.

'No,' said rough McGonagall.

'You are a fool to join zis place, ze rent is ten francs a day, we 'ave to do ze washing up and zen we 'ave to fight ze Arabs.'

The rough Legionnaire broke down and cried. 'I am not what you think,' he said. 'I am a woman.' McGonagall shuddered.

'You're not the Prime Minister of England?' No, she was Molly Nasher, a laundress from Lewisham.

'How did ye get into this fix?'

'It was the tourist agency, they put me on an adventure holiday and I ended up here as laundrywoman to the Commandant.' A bugle call went and all the Legionnaires screamed and ran for their guns.

'And that's only breakfast,' she said. 'At dinner hundreds get killed.'

That night Watson and McGonagall smuggled her over the wall on to a waiting camel.

'Where are you taking me?' she said.

'What would you say to Milton Keynes?' said McGonagall.

'I'd say let's go back to the fort.'

'Do you like dates?' said Dr Watson.

'Yes,' said McGonagall.

'How about July the fourth?'

'Yes,' said McGonagall. 'That sounds like a nice date.'

'Oh, there's plenty more where that came from,' said Dr Watson and reeled off the month of May. 'Boom boom boom boom,' a lone bass drummer was approaching.

'Oh, look who it is,' said McGonagall. 'Gi' us a tune.'

'What would you like to hear?' said the drummer.

'I'd like to hear that my divorce has come through,' said the woman.

'I don't know that,' said the drummer. 'I'll play a selection from Souza.'

'May I have this two-step?' said McGonagall, bowing low. At that moment they were distracted by Arab horsemen who were pulling some prisoners along behind them.

'Hello,' one of the prisoners said. 'We're on the Over Sixty's Adventure Tours from Bradford.' McGonagall laughed as the tourists were dragged screaming away across the rocky desert, all singing 'Roll Out the Barrel'.

Finally, back in London our heroes returned to the office. It was Christmas and heavy snow lay on the slopes of Dolly Parton.

'Do you know what happened while you've been away?' said Miss Moneypenny.

'Yes,' said McGonagall. 'But it was happening to us.' From inside a cupboard came a burst of banjo playing. McGonagall opened the door. There was the nude banjo player.

'What's he doing here?' said McGonagall.

'Can't you see?' said Miss Moneypenny with a withering look. 'He's playing the bloody banjo.'

'Why didn't you call the police?' said Watson running his stethoscope over the nude man's body and banjo.

'Because I felt sorry for him.' Watson put the banjo player under the microscope.

'Yes, you can feel sorry for him but you mustn't feel anything else.'

A rope appeared coming down the chimney followed by a fireman with a parrot on his shoulder.

'What do you want?' said McGonagall.

'Well, actually, I'm looking for the makings of a fire, you see things are pretty quiet at the station, we haven't had a good burn up for over a month.'

'Well, there's no fire here,' said Dr Watson.

'More water Charlie, more water,' said the parrot.

'Look,' said the fireman. 'Would you like me to start a fire? I promise I'll put it out.' Watson put the parrot under the microscope.

95

'More water, Charlie,' it said.

'Who's Charlie?' said McGonagall.

'I am,' said the fireman setting fire to McGonagall's kilt.

'Och, I'm on fire,' screamed McGonagall, trying to beat out the flames.

'More water, Charlie,' said the parrot. Axes smashed in the office door and in poured the fire brigade. In a few moments they had put McGonagall out.

'There,' said the triumphant fireman, 'I feel better now.'

'Well feel this,' said McGonagall and laid him out with a rolling pin.

'More water, Charlie,' said the parrot as McGonagall threw buckets of water over the unconscious figure.

As they carried the unconscious fireman out, he came to and apologised.

'I'm sorry for burning your sporran area,' he said.

'That's all right,' said McGonagall. 'In time they'll grow back.'

'No, they won't,' said Dr Watson. 'You will remain bald in that area for the rest of your life.' McGonagall sobbed, he'd been so proud of his area. 'Is there nothing I can put on it?'

'More water, Charlie,' said the parrot. McGonagall tore a handful of feathers from the parrot's bum.

'Oh, my bum,' said the parrot.

'Oh,' said the fireman. 'He's learned some new words.'

The fire chief took off his helmet and said, 'On behalf of the brigade I'd like to thank you all for a very entertaining afternoon.'

'I'll go back the way I came,' said the fireman with the parrot and climbed up the rope in the chimney. There were cries of 'You bastard', when McGonagall lit a fire in the grate.

'Softee softee catchee monkey.'

'Who are you?' asked Miss Moneypenny to a Chinaman who had entered with a box and said 'Softee softee' etc. The Chinaman gazed with great wisdom through narrowed eyes.

'My name is Fa Kew Tu.'

'Fa Kew Tu?' said McGonagall putting on a fire resistant kilt with built-in agitator.

'Yes,' said the Chinaman. 'I Fa Kew Tu, but you can commence by calling me Fa Kew.'

'Right,' said McGonagall. 'Fa Kew for a start.'

'In Hong Kong Fa Kew Tu very big.'

'Oh yes, Fa Kew Tu, there would be a lot of it in Hong Kong.'

'Will you put that bloody fire out in the grate,' shouted down the fireman.

'Oh,' said the surprised Fa Kew. 'You have talking chimney in England, in China chimney not say anything.' Dr Watson put the Chinese under his microscope.

'This Chinese must be very simple to think we had talking chimneys in England,' and said as much to McGonagall. 'As much,' he said. He took McGonagall to one side while he stood to one as well.

'McGonagall, my friend, this Chinese thinks our chimney speaks, should I tell him the truth and shatter his illusion?'

McGonagall ran the length of the room and back again, stopping only to do several knees-bends and a little twirl. 'There's your answer for him,' he said.

Dr Watson was baffled, biffled and boffled and back to baffled again.

'I no understandee your fliend,' said the Chinese. 'He acts like a clunt.'

By now the fire in the grate had been put out by a gypsy

with a bucket of water who went on to greater things. The Chinese was now the centre of attention, but McGonagall didn't stand too close in case he caught it. It would be terrible at his age to catch Chinese, for a start they did it different ways. In his early days during the Boxer Rebellion, he had seen a Chinese urinating using chopsticks, and a fresh pair every time.

'Look,' said the fireman up the chimney. 'It's getting cold up here, can you relight the fire?' This time Fa Kew was not fooled.

'Ah ha,' he said. 'Chimney no talkee, man uppe chimney talkee.'

The man was a bigger clunt than McGonagall.

'I find most Chinamen fascinating,' said Miss Money-penny.

'I find them mostly in China,' said McGonagall running up to the cupboard and back again. Another baffling moment for all in the room.

'Now, Mr Fa Kew Tu,' said Watson, running his stetho-scope over the Chinaman's chest. 'My fee for that will be five pounds.' The Chinese fainted but recovered immediately as Chinese do. In fact, this was a bit of a Chinese do.

'Solly Fa Kew have no money Solly.'

'My name is not Solly, it is Andrew,' said Watson.

'Solly Andrew,' said Fa Kew.

'You have to pay me, I'm a well-known doctor, I have a practice in Harley Street,' said Solly Watson.

'OK,' said Fa Kew. 'You go have practice in Harley Street and I wait till you come back.'

'He does nae ken,' said McGonagall.

'Yes,' said Fa Kew. 'I know Ken, Ken Livingstone, he my favourite Lem Pee.' He showed Watson his empty wallet.

In time Watson recovered.

'Me Solly no money, what I do?' said Chinese.

'You do the dishes,' said Watson inserting his lunchtime suppository.

The Chinese now started to open his boxes and bundles. He took out a chopstick, placed a plate on top of it and spun it round. It fell to the floor and shattered. He bowed low and put his chopstick away.

'What was all that about?' said McGonagall.

'That was about five minutes,' said the Chinese bowing. 'Now new tlick.' The Chinese spun another plate and broke it.

'I think it's time you went back to Hong Kong,' said Dr Watson.

'No, first I do washing up.' So saying he disappeared into the kitchen. As he did so, the fireman and the parrot came down the chimney. 'You have treated me and my parrot very badly and I'm going to tell my MP.' He was drowned out by the sound of breaking plates coming from the kitchen.

'For God's sake stop him or we'll all be eating off the flae,' said McGonagall. The Chinaman had to be restrained physically from breaking all the crockery. He was a compulsive plate-smasher and for that reason had been deported to England to help the export of Chinese plates. He, in fact, worked for the Chinese secret slervice and had smashed plates right across Gleat Blitain. Watson sat on him while McGonagall tied him up.

'You fool,' said Watson. 'You've tied me to him.'

'I dare not untie the knots or he'll escape,' said McGonagall.

It was a famous court case, made more famous by the fact the prisoner in the witness box was tied to another man called Watson.

'Why,' said the Judge, 'is the Chinaman tied to a doctor?'

'In case the Chinaman needs medical attention,' said the

prosecuting witness McGonagall, who alone knew the combination of the knots.

The fireman gave vital evidence.

'They burnt my parrot's arse,' he said.

'Please,' said the Judge, 'use the word posterior.' The fireman coughed and said, 'Sorry. They burnt my parrot's posterior and arse.'

'Wasn't there a Miss Moneypenny present at the incident?'

'Yes, your majesty,' said McGonagall. 'She's back at the office sticking the plates together for dinner tonight.' Fa Kew Tu got six months and Watson got Hong Kong 'flu. Back at the plate-strewn office, the nude banjo player was plucking 'Old Man Ribber'. He did that sort of thing, many singers let it all hang out, he was no exception.

'What are you doing out of your cupboard?' they all said when they came back.

'Isn't it time you wore some claes?' said the Scots member of the trio.

'No,' said the nude banjo player. 'I come out in a rash.'

'Well come out in that then,' said Miss Moneypenny who was really attracted to the man's method of plucking the strings. She was amazed he wasn't hurt.

'I was saying,' said the fireman, 'I'm going to tell my MP.' He left with his parrot repeating the Chinaman's name. That night they threw caution to the wind and booked a dinner at the Red Star soup kitchen under the arches at Charing Cross. They stood in the queue, McGonagall with a false red beard and Watson with a false nose. They held out their soup bowls.

'Ooooohhhh,' they moaned. 'Pity the poorrrr,' and 'Soupppp, give us soupppp'. As they drew level with the soup pourer he looked closely.

'Ere, your nose 'as just fallen in the soup, I recognise you two, hop it.' A man, well-dressed, patent-leather, highly polished shoes, fine-cut suit and gloves, a cravat with a gold pin and on his fingers several diamond rings, walked along the Embankment whistling an aria from *Faust*, but that didn't last very long and he was soon gone. Such a pity nobody noticed him, not even McGonagall or Dr Watson, but then what good would it have done them if they had seen him. I mean, they didn't know he was an amnesiac millionaire who couldn't remember where he lived. But wait, no dear reader, the man came back. When McGonagall saw him, he said, 'Look, you'll never get any soup dressed like that. Look at us, *we* were turned away.'

The millionaire said, 'I'm sorry if I can't drink soup dressed like this, what do you suggest? I mean, I like soup very much and I should like to know what to wear to drink soup.'

'Well, go hame and wear some old clothes,' said the McScottish chap.

'Well, I can't remember where I live, can you remember?'

'Aye,' said McGonagall, 'No. 6, The Vale . . .' It was a lucky guess. 'Oh, you must come home and have a drink of soup with me.' The amnesiac millionaire tried to hail a taxi but couldn't remember how to.

'I'll do it for ye, Jamie.' It wasn't that easy. The first taxi driver to stop saw Watson's huge false nose.

'No way. I don't take people with false noses.'

'Well,' said McGonagall, 'just let me and this gentleman in, and my friend with the false nose can run alongside.' So that was the arrangement.

'Not so fucking fast,' said Watson belting alongside. What luck, they had made friends with an amnesiac millionaire. As soon as he got to his mansion at No. 6, The Vale, he forgot them.

'Who are you two men and why are you persecuting me

like this? Wait, I remember the soup, of course. I must get ready for the soup. Come in and have some soup.' It was a sumptuous dining room, the table fifty feet long, a butler in livery served them plate after plate of soup. The only thing strange was the millionaire dressed in rags.

'I'm so glad you pointed out the right attire for soup drinking,' the rich man said. 'Look, I want to give you something to help with your soup drinking. Take these two solid silver soup spoons.' So they took them to Joe Cohen the pawnbroker, but there were people ahead. One man was trying to pawn his bed with someone still asleep in it.

'Look, get him out of bed and I'll consider.' The man said the sleeping man was the owner, he had stolen the bed with the owner in it. 'Sorry, no, next please.'

'What would you give us for a soup spoon?' said Watson.

'A bowl of chicken soup.'

'Ha ha ha,' went McGonagall and Watson. 'Very funny Joe. These two spoons are silver.'

Cohen examined the spoons with a jeweller's glass and read out the dreaded words, 'EPNS'. McGonagall fainted first.

'Are you sure?' he said before he hit the flae.

'More water, Charlie.'

'Who said that?' said Watson.

'It's a parrot a fireman pawned this morning.'

McGonagall laid on the flae waiting for the gypsy with the bucket of water.

'I canna wait any longer,' he said, rising from the flae.

'Welcome back to head height,' said Watson racing into the busy street and crying out, 'He has risen.'

'You're a very funny couple,' said Cohen.

'Oh am I? I never knew that before,' said McGonagall late of the flae. Watson raced in back from the street.

'I've told them you have risen,' he said.

'Told who?' said McGonagall the flae.

'The milling throng, the hurrying commuters, passing strangers, the oppressed masses.' The information and a friendly handshake cheered McGonagall. He then enquired of the masses, 'Verily, did they say anything?'

'Fuck all,' said Dr Watson taking a pinch of snuff. Dear friendly Dr Watson whose medications filled half the grave-yards of England. His sneeze that followed was done full in the face of poor Joe Cohen whose face was covered with debris from Watson's last meal which, unfortunately for Cohen, was ham.

'My life, ham,' he wailed, 'that sneeze was anti-Semitic.' From the back of the shop came Rabbi Goldstein with a pledge ticket round his neck. Only that morning his wife had pawned him. The rabbi flicked off the pieces of ham and intoned ancient Hebrew prayers. Watson and McGona-gall were very depressed over the spoons, Watson at 45 degrees and McGonagall at 30.

'Listen boys, my life, don't be so depressed over the spoons. There's an old Jewish saying, it goes, "Don't be so depressed over the spoons".'

Suddenly McGonagall's face lit up.

'Ooooohhh Christ, that hurt,' he said. Dr Watson took more snuff and Cohen took refuge from the coming sneeze.

'I'll make one more appeal to you,' said Watson with a strange flourish of his hat. 'What will you give for these two fine EPNS spoons?'

'I'll give you this,' said Cohen, holding up a piece of wrapping paper. 'Ha ha ha ha.' He was a natural comic.

GROUSE-SHOOTING STREET
PERFORMERS

We now move to the people queuing for their second year outside *The Phantom of the Opera*. Many had died waiting, but there came that pair of life-giving entertainers, all blacked up like minstrels. On the spoons, Sambo McGonagall, on the hat Amos Watson, singing excerpts from *The Phantom of the Opera*.

Watson and McGonagall, The Busking Blackamoors

'Ladies and gentlemen,' said Watson, 'This will save you from the terrible expense of seeing the show.' There and then, Watson and McGonagall, with the spoons rattling at high speed, sang the tender love duet, 'Say You Love Me'. A police constabule approached with his police doggie.

'Pardon me,' he said to our two blackamoors.

'Why?' said blackamoor Watson. 'What have you done?'

''Ave you a licence to street perform?' Of course they had, they were law-abiding citizens.

'We,' said blackamoor McGonagall, 'are law-abiding citizens.'

'I'm sorry, sir,' said the constabule, couching his ear, 'I can't hear a word for your spoons.' The blackamoor Watson shouted to the policeman above the rattle of the spoons, 'Can't stop now.'

'Why not?' shouted the policeman.

'Wuff wuff,' said the police dog.

'The Phantom of the Opera is here,' sang McGonagall.

'Well, I can't see him,' shouted the policeman.

'It's a miracle,' shouted the Pope.

'You see, officer,' shouted Watson. 'He can't stop, he's coming up to the first half finale.'

'He's also coming to Bow Street,' shouted the constabule, pointing to his doggie's teeth. With a great clattering of spoons McGonagall finished the finale, and Watson sped up and down the queue forcing money into his hat. The queue stood and applauded, and the constabule took it as a sign of confidence in the police and took bow after bow. As a finale he made his police dog die for the queen and shake hands. He then sang 'A Policeman's Lot is not a Happy One', with tears streaming down his face.

'You're ruining our pitch,' said McGonagall, mopping it up.

'Now,' said the constabule. 'Can I see your street performer's licence?'

'Of course,' said Amos Watson. 'I have de document here.'

'Hurry up den,' said the police constabule. 'My time in de force is nearly up.' From inside his trousers, Dr Watson whipped out a, wait for it, a piece of purple paper that picked the peck of pepper that Peter Piper picked.

'What does this mean then?' said the constabule. Amos Watson gave a wink and said, 'It's a piece of purple paper that picked the peckle pepper that Peter Piper picked.'

'This man is taking the piss,' thought the policeman as he affixed the doggie to Watson's leg. This encouraged Watson to produce the document.

'This isn't a licence for street performing,' said the policeman. 'It's for grouse shooting.'

'Yes,' said Watson. 'We are grouse-shooting street performers.'

'These men are taking the piss,' thought the policeman, affixing the dog's teeth further up Watson's leg.

'Has that dog got rabies?' said Watson.

'No,' said the police.

'Well, he has the noo,' said McGonagall.

'I shall have to confiscate those spoons,' shouted the policeman as McGonagall started the Overture shouting, 'Beginners please.'

'We're all beginners here,' shouted the queue. With a dextrous move the policeman removed one of McGonagall's spoons leaving him jerking in mid-air with nae sound.

'You'll go blind,' said a short-sighted well-wisher. But abandoning the single spoon, McGonagall snatched out Watson's false teeth and did a fantastic fandango up and down the queue using the teeth as castanets.

'I will charge you with reporting to Bow Street tomorrow with the other spoon and a brace of grouse. Now for the police Christmas lucky draw.' So saying he emptied the money from Watson's hat into his pocket. 'And a Merry Christmas from the force,' he concluded.

'Och, you've ruined our living,' said McGonagall.

'Yes, you've ruined their living,' echoed the queue. The people in the queue rose as one man, because it was only one man.

Next morning McGonagall and Watson reported to Bow Street. They had travelled about a quarter of a mile by British Rail and were now broken men. 'Ah,' said the constabule.

'I see you are British Rail victims,' he said to the men in a heap on the flae. 'Weren't you two blackamoors last night?' he said. McGonagall put his hand up the back of Watson's jacket and made him say 'Yes. It was the only way we could get through Brixton.'

'Now,' said the policeman. 'Where are the grouse?'

'They're in Scotland,' said McGonagall and handed him two grouse eggs. 'There you are, constabule,' he said. 'All you have to do is wait till they hatch.'

'I can't wait,' said the policeman and swallowed them. 'Delicious,' he said.

'Now,' said the policeman taking up a pose. 'Would either of you two like to confess to the Jack the Ripper murders?'

'Why?' said McGonagall.

'Why?' said the policeman. 'It would further my career.'

'More water, Charlie.'

'Who said that?' said Watson.

'Oh that,' said the constabule. 'That's a parrot that's been handed in by a rabbi.'

'Now there's a good meal for you,' said McGonagall. 'What would you say to parrot and chips?'

Sitting on McGonagall's knee, Watson said, 'A gottle of gear, a gottle of gear.'

'Stop this ventriloquist,' said the constabule. 'You are not fooling me, I know there are two of you.'

'More water, Charlie.'

'I'll have to go and shut the parrot up.'

The Dick Tracy two-way watch activated.

'Listen, you two go to Ireland,' said the voice.

'Why, why us?' said McGonagall. 'Gottle of gear.'

'The whole idea is to get you out of danger lurking. There's a lot in London whereas Ireland is lurk-free.' Economy was essential said McGonagall, as they both rowed out of Fishguard Harbour with nothing as a navigational aid other than a canary. 'If the air gets bad he'll fall off,' said McGonagall rowing, straining and farting. They reached mid-channel when a U-boat surfaced.

'We're being followed,' said Watson.

'Aye,' said McGonagall. 'You see, that's a prize canary, it won Crufts.'

'Isn't that a dog show?' said Watson.

'Yes, we just won it on persistence.' The conning tower of the submarine opened, a captain came out with a boat hook.

'Hands up, don't try anything funny or zer canary gets it.' Our heroes were stinned (stinned).

'Don't be funny, you say,' they said. 'Can you tell us how to be funny in a rowing boat in the middle of the Irish Sea?'

'Yes, I can,' said the captain. He immediately put on a funny nose, dropped his trousers and said, 'I say, I say, I say, vy does Hitler wear red, white and blue braces? To hold up his trousers, ya, ha ha ha ha. Now it's your turn.'

'I say, what has eight wheels and flies?' said McGonagall.

'I don't know,' said Watson. 'What has eight wheels and flies?'

'Two corporation dust carts,' said McGonagall.

'Good,' said the captain. 'You are prisoners of zer German Navy.'

'The war is over,' said McGonagall.

'Yes, it's over here,' said the captain.

'And a gottle of gear,' said Watson, trying to disguise himself as a dummy.

'Ach, zen ve must surrender to you, vot are your orders?' said the captain. McGonagall gave them.

'Two shepherd's pies, then prunes and custard, that and a tow to Ireland.' Dawn on the Irish coast as our two heroes were dropped ashore.

'A top of the morning to you,' said an Irish drunk being sick in a jaunting cart. 'Welcome to Scotland.'

'This is Ireland,' said McGonagall, the funnier of the two.

'Scotland?' said the Irishman. 'Den I've come too far,' and he jaunted off into the sea.

'Psttt.' The sound came from behind a bush over there.

'Pssssttt.' A figure emerged, a man in an Irish hat carrying a shillelagh.

'Psssttt, don't tell the missus, I'm your contact.'

'Psssttt' came from behind another bush, in fact, all the bushes were 'Pssstttingggg'. This was the massed Irish Pssstttinnnggg secret service.

'Oh, dere's a lot of us,' said the Irishman in the kilt. 'First, have you got a canary?' McGonagall triumphantly drew the cage from under his kilt. Unfortunately, part of him was trapped in the bars and he let out a scream. 'AAAAARRRRRRRGGGGGGHHHHHHHH.'

'Sssshhhhh,' said the Irishman.

'Psssttt,' said the bushes.

'Dat canary is a rare one stolen from Dublin Castle,' said the Irishman. 'It was kidnapped by Arab extremists and held captive until we left Yasser Arafat having his photo taken with the Pope playing hockey. How did you come by this

rare canary? It must have taken great courage, skill, planning
and a daring raid to carry it out. Tell us how you grappled
hand to hand with Arab agents. Tell us all.'

'Well,' said McGonagall. 'I went in a shop and bought it.'
The Irish drew back, forwards, sideways, then back again.

'Was it a plant?'

'No,' said McGonagall. 'It was a canary.' The Irishman
was stunned.

'It's a miracle,' said the Pope.

'Look, dere's a reward for de return of dis canary here.
It's a week's holiday here in Ireland.'

'Where in Ireland?' said McGonagall.

'Right here, where you're standing. A whole week here,' said the Irishman.

'There's not much doing here,' said McGonagall.

'Oh, wait until tonight, everybody's doing it, you have to watch where you tread, and if you're bored there's always the tide.'

'Where do we eat?' said Watson.

'Oh, you can eat here, all you got to do is get some food here.'

'Ppppsssttt,' came from behind a bush.

'Ah, dat's Inspector Ryan pssssttting, dat's the signal for us ter take you to Dublin Castle to be personally thanked by the Prime Minister.'

'And that is our signal that we're not coming,' said McGonagall with a gesture. Rowing back was in the teeth of heavy winds from Watson. McGonagall took it in turns to row, when he'd finished his turn he started his turn again, and so it went on. Every now and then, to encourage McGonagall, Watson said 'God, you look lovely in the moonlight Amanda.'

Rowing and gottle of gearing, they persisted in the teeth of the gale. The exhausted McGonagall, still taking it in turns to row himself, arrived at the Port of London Authority's jetty.

'Give us a hand, please,' he pleaded.

'What for?' said the jettymaster. 'You've got two of your own, why do you want a third?'

'It would help with my juggling act,' said McGonagall.

'Heave to,' said the jettymaster, so McGonagall heaved two at him and laid him out.

With loving care they searched the jettymaster's pockets and were well pleased with it.

'What are you men doing here?' said a passing customs officer.

'We are pre-death morticians,' said Watson, 'and we are just measuring one of our future clients.'

'How is business?' said the customs officer.

'Not very good,' said McGonagall, taking the jetty-master's inside leg measurement with great care. 'This was the first one today and even he is not quite ready.'

'It sounds a very good idea,' said the customs officer. 'When the time comes, could you do me?'

'Yes, a very wise choice,' said McGonagall and hurled two at him.

'Once again,' said McGonagall. 'Into the pockets, once again,' quoting *Henry V, Part One*.

'What do we do now?' said Watson.

'Well, the first thing we do is not wait here for *Henry V, Part Two*,' said McGonagall. McGonagall stopped a taxi.

'Do you sell beer?' said McGonagall.

'No,' said the taxi driver.

'Then you're no good to me,' said McGonagall.

'How about a gottle of gear?' said Watson.

'I just told you, I don't sell the stuff,' said the taxi driver.

'No, that wasn't me,' said Watson. 'That was my friend using me as a ventriloquist's dummy.'

'Well, here's me using you as a punchbag,' said the taxi driver, and let him have one. Drawn to this new trade, McGonagall immediately measured him, and started on a trial grave. Alas! Watson regained consciousness as the first spadeful of earth fell on him. As he rose from the shallow grave, a gasp went up from the crowd. 'He has risen,' they gasped.

'It's a miracle,' said the Pope.

'A bottle of beer,' said Watson. 'Thank God I'm cured.' He reshagged his pipe. He had been a pipe smoker for many years and to stop the craving he bent anchors. He took them home to his wife who said, 'What can we do

'He has risen,' gasped the crowd

with these?' He made some stunning suggestions to her. One was that on sunny days they would take them to Beachy Head and drop them on sunbathers. Eventually he straightened them out and gave them back to the Navy to re-bend. They honoured him with an afternoon of horn-piping aboard the *Cutty Sark* in Greenwich. He never forgave them.

'I see, what got you on to anchors then?' said McGona-gall.

'I was deprived of them as a child,' said Dr Watson. 'There was never one in the house when I needed it, and my father took his own automatic one to the office. You see, he worked in an office on a cliff where the windows were always kept open. In the terrible gales of 1980 every single clerk was blown out of the building except him. It was all on account of his anchor.'

'That was a very moving story,' said McGonagall.

'Yes, I had to move about a bit, it was getting chilly,' said Watson.

CHAPTER NINETY-TWO

Back at the office they were greeted by Miss Moneypenny, who in the meantime had married the nude banjo player.

'Er, has anyone seen my parrot?' said the fireman.

'We planned to have children,' said Miss Moneypenny.

'That's splendid,' said McGonagall with a twirl and a tickle. 'I have the plans for a child in here,' he said. 'If anyone knows the combination of the safe.'

'Yes, turn knob to right,' said Miss Moneypenny, and McGonagall had to think about that. How silly of him, of course she meant the knob on the door of the safe. Any other would be painful. He swung open the giant safe door. Out stepped the YMCA manager.

'What about this bill?' he said.

'If those are the plans for a child,' said Miss Moneypenny, 'I'm going to keep a Rottweiler.'

'Look,' said McGonagall addressing the YMCA man, who had attached his hands to his throat. To allow the manager better purchase Watson raised the YMCA man higher, making a delightful tableau, which Miss Moneypenny photographed.

'Have you ever travelled free by air?' said McGonagall.

'No,' said the manager.

'Well, here you go then,' said McGonagall and they

'What about this bill?'

threw him out of the window. He landed on the roof of a hold-up, get-away car and wondered why he spent the next six months in jail.

Back in the office they examined the plans of a child.

'There,' said McGonagall. 'All you have to do is start it.

Just press the button here.' The child started at the first touch.

'It's the new Nissan Autochild, available in all good stores,' he said.

'But it's Japanese,' said Miss Moneypenny. 'I don't want a nip child.'

'Then,' said McGonagall, 'you must stay away from nips.' There was a quick burst of banjoing from the nude banjo player.

'Is he still in the cupboard?' said Watson, peering through the keyhole and not liking what he saw.

'Yes,' said Miss Moneypenny. 'He spent the honeymoon in there.'

'You must love him very much,' said Watson. 'It cannot be easy in a cupboard.'

'No, but we had our moments.'

'Did not the banjo get in the way?' said McGonagall.

'No,' she said. 'He just played straight through it, he's a very good string plucker,' said Miss Moneypenny.

'Yes,' said McGonagall. 'I knew one who did pheasants.'

'What we need in this office are some games,' said McGonagall.

'Do you like draughts?'

'Yes,' said Miss Moneypenny.

'Good,' said McGonagall opening a window. Watson puffed on his pipe, smiled and then said, 'I spy with my little eye something beginning with A.'

'Oh, good luck to you,' said McGonagall. 'I hope you'll be very happy with it.'

'You silly Scotsman,' said Watson. 'That was a game, you have to guess what I've seen, beginning with A.'

'Right,' said McGonagall. 'A table, a chair, and a window.'

'Oh,' said Watson. 'You've played this game before.'

At that moment a huge fat man squeezed himself through the window. 'I'm sorry about this,' he said. 'But I couldn't get through the front door.'

'Oh, that's a pity,' said McGonagall. 'That's what we made it for.'

'My name is James Thirk,' said the fat man.

'Good, we'll let you know and have a nice day,' said McGonagall.

'I haven't finished,' said the fat man.

'Well I have,' said McGonagall.

'Wait,' said the kindly Dr Watson, refilling his pipe. 'Something tells me this fat man needs help.'

'He doesn't need help, he needs a crane,' said McGonagall.

'No,' said the fat man. 'I'm heavy enough without a crane. That would make it impossible for me even to get through the windows. Don't laugh,' the fat man continued. 'I'm here to sell you slimming tablets.'

'I think,' said McGonagall, 'you're in the wrong job, Jamie.'

'What company makes these tablets?'

'Insta-thin,' said the fat man.

'I've got a better name for it, how about Bloat-a-body?' said McGonagall.

'How much do you weigh?' said McGonagall circling the huge mass.

'Thirty-three stone,' said the man as the floor gave way. There was a knock at the door and a very worried bank manager entered.

'Look, your legs are hanging through our ceiling,' he said.

'They are nae my legs,' said McGonagall. 'As you can see, I have both mine up here with me. No, the man you are looking for is Mr James Thirk, travelling salesman with Insta-thin.'

'I know he's a traveller, he's travelled through our ceiling,' said the manager, at which moment the bloated body went through the floor.

'He's all yours now,' said McGonagall. 'And can we have our carpet back?'

'Are you all right down there?' shouted McGonagall in a friendly voice, and throwing down the man's hat.

The nude banjo player came out of the cupboard and displayed strongly. 'Your honeymoon's done you a power of good,' said McGonagall. 'I can see the marks.'

'Look,' said the nude banjo player, giving a quick pluck on his instrument. 'We're still on our honeymoon, this is only the third day.'

'Oh,' said Dr Watson, who knew about such things. 'You'll never last the week, man, you've got the first sign of Swonnicles.'

'Swonnicles?' said the nude banjo player, with a dangerous pluck. 'What are they?'

'They are the gradual movement of parts,' said Dr Watson, who knew about these things.

'Did I leave my pills up there?' shouted the fat man from down below.

'No, they went down with you,' said Dr Watson, who knew about such things. 'There's a crane coming to take you home,' he said. The great crowd stood in awe as the great crane pulled the bloated body through the window taking half the wall with it. 'Oh deary me,' groaned the great crowd. 'Are you open for business?'

'No, we're open to the sky,' said the bank manager. 'And there's a huge overdraft coming in.' The press arrived with cameras, tripods, microphones, and for some reason a cucumber.

'Mr Collington,' said a journalist. 'Did you see the body of Mr Thirk?'

'No, most of it was out of sight behind him,' said McGonagall. 'But people said there was still a lot of him there.'

'Was it an IRA plot?' said the journalist.

'No, but if they did have a plot for him it would have to be very big and very deep,' said McGonagall.

'Is Mr Thirk in great danger?' asked the journalist.

'Yes,' said McGonagall.

'Of what?' asked the journalist.

'Exploding,' said McGonagall.

'I took some of those slimming pills,' said a female voice.

'Where are you?' said McGonagall.

'That's what I want to know,' said the woman. A journalist drew nigh to Dr Watson.

'Are Mr Thirk's parents still alive?'

'Not really, they live in Milton Keynes.' The journalist drew nigh again.

'How many children did they have?'

'They had twelve and he was eight of them,' said Watson.

'What was the cucumber for?' said the drew-nigh journalist.

'It's for eating,' said a cameraman. 'And can I have a picture of Mr McGonagall by the hole in the floor, and then one of the hole in the floor by him?' A journalist drew nigh.

'Was Mr Thirk happily married?'

'Whenever she could get out from under him, yes.' By now the huge Mr Thirk had been loaded on to an articulated lorry.

'Where do I take 'im?' said the lorry driver.

'Heathrow,' said McGonagall.

'Which part?' said the driver.

'All of it,' said McGonagall.

'Was Mr Thirk under a doctor?' said a journalist.

'No,' said the bank manager. 'But we think there's a doctor under him.'

'What are we going to do with the hole in the floor?' said Miss Moneypenny.

'I think for the time being we should leave it where it is.'

From below, the bank manager shouted up, 'Mr McGonagall you can't go on wearing the kilt. All my lady staff are very agitated.'

'Well,' said McGonagall. 'Tell them nae to look up.' The manager wrung his hands.

'But it's compulsive viewing, they are bringing their friends in to see, people are saying it's better than *EastEnders* and *Neighbours*.' McGonagall felt a warm glow go through him.

'I'll try not to stand too near the edge,' he promised, but he lied in his teeth. Every morning when the bank opened, McGonagall did several inspiring leaps across the hole singing 'My love is like a red red rose'. The offers of marriage flowed in. One woman secreted herself under McGonagall's bed. She was a fifty-five-year-old, one-legged spinster, Rebecca Goldsmith.

'Oh William, I seen you through the hole in your ceiling,' she said.

McGonagall was fascinated as she hopped around the room singing Jewish love songs.

'Marry me,' she said on the hop.

'But you're Jewish, you're not allowed to marry outside the faith.'

She hopped into the kneeling position by his bed, bonging the po.

'You can become Jewish,' she said.

'No,' he said, grabbing the blankets up to him. 'I'm not going to have that done to me. There's mair to mickle where snickle gaes wrang.'

'I won't cost you much,' she pleaded. 'You only have to buy me one shoe at a time.'

'How did she get in here?' said McGonagall, cowering in a corner.

'The security guards let her in,' said Watson from his chest of drawers bed.

'But there's nae security guards,' said McGonagall.

'Ah well, there you go,' said Watson. 'That's how she got in.'

'Right, can you get her out the same way,' said McGonagall.

'Look,' she said. 'I've got a very nice rabbi, he doesn't hurt.'

'Nae,' said McGonagall. 'I've got a rabbi, Rabbi Burns (Frank Carson, 1926–81).

'Listen,' said the Jewish one-legger. 'I'm very very rich.'

'Och, let me slip this little rubber band on your engagement finger to show my undying love and trust on your account,' said McGonagall.

'She's leading you up the garden path,' said Watson.

'No she's not, she's kneeling by the bed, can you no see, Jamie, you silly silly Sassenach?' said McGonagall. It was quite amazing how Watson in his bed in the chest of drawers thought that he, McGonagall and the one-legged Jewish girl were walking up a garden path. It was only then that he heard the empty bottle fall from Watson's nerveless fingers to the flae, and the whispered words of 'Famous Grouse' as they came wafting on the warm night air.

'Bong' went the po, as Rebecca struck it again.

'Bong.'

'Two o'clock,' said Watson as another empty bottle hit the ground. Clang it went.

'One o'clock,' said McGonagall. 'You must be going home my darling to get ready for our wedding day.'

121

'More water, Charlie.'

'Who said that?' said McGonagall.

'Oh dear,' said Watson. 'I forgot to tell you.'

'More water, Charlie,' it went again.

'Oh, my life,' said the one-legger. 'There's a woman in the house already and us only engaged two minutes!'

'Dear heart,' said the lying bastard McGonagall. 'It's only a parrot from the fire brigade.' Watson coughed, nearly emptying himself. Who would believe that this *wasn't* a fire brigade parrot but an actual woman he had picked up saying the words 'More water, Charlie' who was now talking in her sleep in the drawer below him. The woman climbed out of the bottom drawer. She had a face like W. C. Fields turned inside out. McGonagall only screamed for twenty minutes when he saw her.

'Oh, I'm not that ugly,' said the crone.

'I've not finished screaming yet,' said McGonagall.

'Do you know this woman?' said Rebecca. Bong.

'Och, it's a woman, is it?' said McGonagall.

'Don't laugh, I've just been given a face lift.'

'I'm glad I wasn't in the lift with you,' said McGonagall.

'She's got a kind face,' said Dr Watson.

'Yes, the wrong kind,' said McGonagall.

'More water, Charlie,' she said. Watson took her to the bathroom. It was a very simple job of fixing a hose to her mouth and tying her in the bath. There was a struggling sound and four men brought something in.

'What does it do?' said McGonagall.

'It doesn't do anything,' said the men. 'It just stays there.'

'Let me see the label,' said McGonagall. 'A Knirt? I never ordered a Knirt.'

'No, it was me,' said Watson. 'I saw it in *The Exchange and Mart* and I couldn't resist it. It was this or an electric turkey, and I thought of the two this would be safer.'

122

'What are those lumps on it?' said McGonagall.

'They're knirt lumps,' said Dr Watson. 'You see, basically, it's a jelly detector. If there's a jelly in the house it sets off an alarm and a black cloud of smoke.'

'Is it switched on?' said McGonagall.

'More than I am,' said Watson pressing a small button. Immediately a cloud of smoke rose from the top of the Knirt filling the room.

'My God,' said McGonagall. 'There must be a jelly in the house.' A frantic search started for the jelly. When all hope was almost lost, McGonagall spotted it in the bottom of the fridge.

'Quick, throw it out of the window,' said Watson as the Knirt siren woke the neighbourhood. The ejected jelly had landed on the upturned helmet of Constable Morrison, who donned it before realising. He was at that time handcuffed to a felon.

'Is this your jelly, sir?' asked the constabule, as McGonagall opened the door.

'Yes, but for God's sake don't bring it in, it sets off the smoke alarm.'

'Would you blow into this green bag, sir?' said the constabule.

'Hurry up,' said the handcuffed felon. 'I want to get to my cell.'

When the bag showed negative, the policeman burst into tears.

'I was pinning my hopes on a double arrest tonight,' he said.

'There, there,' said McGonagall, patting him on the jelly. 'The night is still young. Listen,' he said. The streets of London were alive with old street cries. Sure enough, came the distant calls of 'You bastard', 'I'll get you for this', 'Help', 'Murder', 'Pakistanis out', etc. It brought a look of cheer to the constabule's face and the roses back to his knees.

'Are we going to be here all fucking night?' said the felon.

'Patience, my man,' said the policeman, splitting his head open with a truncheon.

'Sod this,' said the felon.

'Now, sir, is this your jelly?' he said again, holding up the upturned helmet. McGonagall took one of his EPNS spoons from out of his nightshirt. He took a taste.

'Yes,' he said. 'That tastes like my jelly.'

'Anybody could say that,' said the constabule.

'Anybody just did,' said McGonagall. This brilliant wit silenced the policeman, but his benzedrine inhaler soon restored him to fighting strength in the force.

'You tell me whose jelly this tastes like,' said McGonagall, passing him a spoon.

After a quick taste the constabule said, 'That tastes like Tesco's to me, sir.'

'Here, I'll have a taste,' said the felon, taking the spoon.

'That's a Sainsbury's,' he finally concluded.

'Have you,' said the constabule, 'got a receipt for this jelly?'

'Yes, but it's with my accountant, and my accountant says it came from Safeways. Look, officer,' said McGonagall, 'if I eat it all here, would that satisfy you?'

'Yes, because I would then be able to put my helmet back on.'

At that moment the overflow pipe from the bathroom began to run into the street.

'It looks like you need a plumber,' said the constabule.

'No, no,' said McGonagall. 'I can manage to eat it without a plumber.'

McGonagall scooped the helmet clean, licked the spoon

124

and returned it in its paper wrapping into his nightshirt pocket.

'Well, sir, I'll be getting along,' said the policeman.

'You'll be getting a long what?' said McGonagall.

'Come on,' said the felon. 'Can't you see he's a nutter?' There was the sound of one leg coming downstairs.

'Come, my darling,' said Rebecca. 'What is it, constabule? Is my beloved in trouble with the police? Oh, it's Constable Morrison, you remember me, I played the one-legged Cinderella in the police pantomime.'

'Yes,' said the constable. 'I see you still have it. It must be a great comfort to you.'

'I don't believe this,' said the felon. 'I'll be glad when I'm inside.'

'Not as glad as me,' said the constabule, splitting his head open again.

THE GREAT
CRYSTAL PALACE TERE

Dr Watson got out his Skoda, it had been on blocks for four years and knackered for five. They said he drove a hard bargain, and there it was parked in the gutter. Like some women on their wedding night, it wouldn't turn over.

'It's the distributor,' said McGonagall from under his bonnet.

'Oh, wait till I get the bastard,' said Watson.

'I can't wait that long,' said McGonagall. 'It's no good, we'll have to call the A A man.' An A A man came. (Eh?) He didn't mend the car, but they all felt much better when he left. In a blinding snowstorm McGonagall and Watson arrived at the ancestral home.

'Och my son, my son,' said his mother, embracing Watson.

'I'm over here, Mither,' said McGonagall.

'Oh, you've changed,' said his mither.

'Yes, the other pair wore out,' said McGonagall.

'Och now,' said the mither. 'Let me have a good look at you.' She had a good look at him and fainted. But she soon came round as they massaged her head with whisky.

'Och, there's nothing like the old remedy,' she said, sinking half a bottle.

'Och, Mrs McGonagall. You should be proud of your son,' said Watson.

'I know,' she said. 'But why aren't I?'

'And who are you, you ugly-looking bastard?' said Mrs McGonagall to Watson.

'I, madam, am a doctor of medicine,' said Watson. 'And who are you, you ugly-looking bastard?' he said to her. Just then the father came in out of the snae with his bagpipes at the ready, which he played despite the haemorrhoids, the hernia and the hots for Madonna.

'Come here and warm yourself by this haggis,' she said. 'It was only shot this morning.'

'Och, it's nae so hot,' said McGonagall.

'You're nae so hot yourself,' said Mither.

'Och aye,' said his exhausted father. 'You'll nae hear bagpipe playing like that outside of Scotland.'

'Thank God for that,' said Watson, making for England. As they sat and ate fresh thistles and grummocks, they caught up with all the family news. Most of them were caught evading the police.

'Och, have you heard from Grannie McGonagall?' asked William.

The straining Fither

'Not since she died,' said Mither, forcing another thistle down his throat. With great straining and farting the father blew up the bagpipes again. They wailed into life along with several postern blasts. Finally, scarlet in the face, he said, 'What would you like me to play?'

'Outside,' said William.

'What?' said his father. 'It's terrible out there.'

'It sounds bloody terrible in here as well,' said William.

'Mrs McGonagall,' said Dr Watson. 'I'd like to compliment you on your cooking, but I can't find any reason for it.'

'Och,' said the steaming piper. 'This is the lament I played over my poor father's grave.'

'Well,' said William. 'I can't wait for somebody to play it over yours.'

'Och Mither, I've got wonderful news,' said McGonagall.

'Och son,' she said. 'That sounds like wonderful news.'

'Yes Mither, I'm going to do something you've always wanted me to do,' said McGonagall.

'Well, hurry up,' she said. 'We'll all wait while you do it and I'll open the window.'

'I've promised myself to another,' he said.

'Oh, that's gude,' she said. 'I think I'll have another one too.'

She poured one and threw back a Famous Grouse.

'Oh,' said Watson. 'How long have you had that grouse?' he said, as it flew past his head.

'Och, we caught it in the crankies this morning,' she said.

'I've often been caught by them myself,' said Watson nostalgically. He then stood very slowly, rapped on the table with a spoon and said, 'Ladies and gentlemen, pray silence for the singer,' and in a deep trembling baritone sang 'Swanee Ribber'. He came to a trembling high-note finish. He sat down to a sullen silence and a plate of porridge full in the face.

'We could have done without all that,' said Mither.

'So could I,' said Watson. 'It's bad enough him playing bagpipes at the same time.'

'Now, Mither,' said McGonagall through the howling of the pipes. 'What would you say to a one-legged daughter-in-law?'

'I'd say where's the other one?' she said.

'How many daughters-in-law do you want?' said McGonagall.

'I've got nothing against a one-legged woman,' said

128

Mither. 'Come to think about it, neither has she.'

'I must tell you, Mither, she's one of the Hebrew persuasion,' said McGonagall.

'Thank God,' said Mither. 'So long as she's not Jewish.'

'Excuse me, Mrs McGonagall, you ignorant bastard,' said Watson, and he explained.

'I'm getting the drift of it,' said Mither.

'Well, it wasn't me,' said the farting piper. Then with a strange gargling sound Father collapsed in a heap on his groaning pipes that gradually deflated with a long moan.

'Is that him or his pipes?' said the frantic McGonagall.

'Do nay worry,' said the mither, pouring half a bottle of Highland Mist down the father's throat, and reinflated the bladder with bulging cheeks, steaming head and more postern blasts.

'What's wrong with you marrying a Scottish highland lass?' Mither raged.

'Well, they've nearly all got it,' said McGonagall. 'Don't you remember the treatment?'

'Believe me,' said Dr Watson through the hell of it. 'She is a fine upstanding girl.'

'Well, with one leg, that's all she can do,' said Mither spitting in the fire and sending sheets of flame up the chimney. 'Is she pretty?' said the mither.

'Well, nae exactly pretty,' said McGonagall. 'More like ugly.'

'Have we nae enough ugly people in the family?' said the mither.

'No,' said McGonagall. 'That's why I'm marrying her. Her father is very wealthy.'

'Then why don't you marry him?' she said. The piper let go another one, which knocked off Watson's hat.

'Och, he's got a lot going for him,' said McGonagall.

'Yes,' said Watson. 'And it's all going over here.'

'Can you support her?' said Mither.

'Aye, if I stand on the side where the leg's missing,' said McGonagall.

'Does this leg run in the family?' said Mither.

'No, they all have to hop,' said McGonagall.

'The fire needs seeing to, Mither,' said the steaming piper. So with a lightning quick swig she let another one go.

'Your chimney's on fire,' came a startled voice from outside.

'Oh, that's good,' she said. 'That'll warm the house. Now, are ye all staying to dinner?'

'Yes,' they said.

'Well you can stay,' she said. 'But there isn't any.'

'The wedding will take place in the reformed synagogue,' said McGonagall.

'What's wrang with the local kirk?' said Mither.

'They've sold it,' said McGonagall.

'What is it now?' said Mither.

'It's the reformed synagogue,' he said.

'Who's giving the beautiful bride away?' said the steaming piper.

'Och,' said McGonagall. 'It's too late for that, everybody knows. Here is a photograph of the bride,' he said holding it up.

'But that's a carthorse,' said Mither.

'Aye,' said McGonagall. 'But it'll have to do. Photographs are expensive.'

'How many children are ye going tae have?' said Mither.

'Me? None,' said the startled McGonagall. 'But she's agreed to have three. We were going to have five but they say that every fifth child born in the world is Chinese.'

OOOOHHHH, IT WAS A GREAT THREE-LEGGED WEDDING

It was a great wedding as the three-legged couple stood at the altar before Rabbi Guts.

'Now do you, William McGonagall, take this woman to be your lawful wedded wife?' he asked.

'Of course I dae,' said McGonagall. 'That's why I brought her here.'

Meanwhile, outside, Watson sat in the get-away car with the bride's dowry in the boot.

'And do you, Rebecca, promise to stay beside this man for the rest of your life?'

'Yes, he's too fast for me. He has a leg advantage.'

'More water, Charlie.'

'Who said that?' said McGonagall.

'It's the schule parrot,' said the rabbi. 'We use him to keep burglars away.'

'More water, Charlie,' said the parrot.

'Look,' said the rabbi who had a bad attack of them. 'Can you all come back tomorrow?'

'What about the honeymoon?' said the bride.

'You can have that this afternoon in a room at the YWCA when the last couple have finished.'

'Yes,' said the bride, 'but they might run overtime.'

'Don't worry,' said the rabbi. 'There's a warning bell when there's five minutes to go.'

'How long do they give you?' said McGonagall.

'Twenty minutes,' said the rabbi. 'However many times you do it in the time is up to you.'

'But it takes fifteen minutes to get that wooden leg off,' said McGonagall. 'That only leaves five.'

'Oh my life,' said the rabbi. 'Then you'll have to apply for an extension.'

'Look,' said the best man. 'Does anybody want me any longer?'

The rabbi looked him up and down.

'Not any longer, no, five foot eleven, that's as long as any man needs to be, and good luck with the molesting.'

'If anyone has an objection to this marriage, let them speak now or for ever hold his piece.'

'Five to two, it won't last,' said a Jewish voice.

'Eleven to four on,' said another.

'Evens,' said yet another.

'All right, I'll be taking bets in the vestry after the service,' said the rabbi.

'Call this a service,' said a voice. 'I've been here half an hour and I haven't even had a bowl of chicken soup.'

'You should speak,' said the rabbi. 'I've found so many buttons in the collection plate, it's a wonder your clothes didn't fall off.'

McGonagall waved a white handkerchief in the rabbi's face. 'Remember us?' he said. 'We came here to get married.'

'Oh, I thought you were surrendering,' said the rabbi taking the handkerchief and blowing his nose. 'This is the last time I have a Jewish wedding,' said McGonagall.

'The last? My life, I thought this was your first. Are you a bigamist?'

The bride started to cry.

'What's the matter?' said McGonagall.

'That was my handkerchief,' she said.

'There, there, sorry my dear,' said the rabbi, handing it back to her full of it.

'More water, Charlie.'

In the schule, the rabbi was putting a rubber band around the parrot's beak so the wedding could proceed.

'Now,' said the rabbi. 'For hygienic reasons the rest of the service will take place outside. Now, who will give the bride away?' McGonagall raised his arms, his fingers clawing the air. 'For God's sake,' he said, 'nobody give her away until after the honeymoon. By then it will have healed up.' The bride's father put a thermal capel on.

'I give my daughter's hand, part of the forearm and other essential pieces in marriage. I bring him into the House of Israel with an option to buy.'

'Are we married yet?' said McGonagall.

'Now,' said the rabbi, 'we come to the sacred part where you place a silver coin between the bride's teeth, as a sign of your undying love.' As a sign of not having the money McGonagall fainted to the flae. But after another bucket of water he was soon his old self again. Skint.

'All right,' said the rabbi. 'If you've no silver, something shiny will do.' McGonagall reached deep into his kilt. With a scream he pulled out a silver safety-pin; pulling the hair off he placed it between her teeth. The one-legged bride tottered.

'He's too old for her,' said an insurer's voice.

McGonagall drew himself up. 'I'll have you all know, I have the body of a boy of eighteen.'

'Where do you keep it?' said a voice.

'More water, Charlie.'

'Oh,' said the rabbi. 'He's broken the rubber band.'

'Never mind that,' said the bride's father. 'This wedding is going to break me.' He pulled out the linings of his pockets.

'Please no,' pleaded the rabbi. 'Not the white-eared

133

elephant. Last time you did that the congregation didn't come back for a month.'

'That was jealousy.' A distant dog barked. 'I'll get him,' thought McGonagall.

'A solemn moment,' said the rabbi. 'Will the bride and bridegroom hold hands.'

'Not without gloves,' said the bride's mother. 'We don't want her to catch it.' The rabbi raised his arms releasing two jets of steam.

'Now, the giving of gifts.'

'We give a set of fish knives,' said the bride's mother.

'And we', said McGonagall's mother, 'have given a set of freshly laundered bedsheets with stains nae visible to the naked eye.'

'Now,' said the rabbi. 'A silver collection for the happy couple.' A groan of horror went through the congregation, many climbed out of windows.

'Remember,' said the rabbi. 'This is God's house.'

'No, it isn't,' said a broker's voice. 'It's with the Bradford and Bingley.'

'Order, please, order,' said the rabbi.

'Order? Order?' said a schmutter voice. 'I haven't had an order this month.' The rabbi turned the pages of the Torah, an unpaid gas bill fell out.

'Oh,' he groaned.

The rabbi turned the pages of the Torah; a photo of Madonna fell out.

'Oooohhh,' said the rabbi. 'This is the work of Arab terrorists.' Watson strolled up the aisle.

'The wedding dowry is false,' said Watson. 'These fish knives are EPNS.'

The rabbi turned to the bride and took the cover off. 'You still want to marry him?'

'Only just,' she said. The groom's father had suddenly

started again on the bagpipes. The policeman picked him up bodily, not without difficulty. Policemen's trousers, like all council buildings, have no ballroom.

'More water, Charlie.'

'I now pronounce you man and wife,' said the rabbi.

'Are we man and wife?' said the one-legged bride.

'Well,' said the rabbi. 'Let's put it like this: he's a man but you're not. It's up to you.'

'Up to me?' said the bride. 'I've had it up to here.'

'Oh,' said the rabbi. 'I must meet him one day.'

At the wedding breakfast of chicken liver and thistles, McGonagall gave his speech as a poem:

> Oooohhhhh wonderful wedding day,
> Is the finest one they say.
> Never mind what other people say,
> I say it's a very nice day.

An hour later the happy couple were at the YWCA in the queue for the honeymoon bed. Couples were already at the door hammering for admission, sobs, groans and sighs coming from within.

'The bill is still unpaid for the YMCA,' said that manager.

'This is the YWCA,' said McGonagall.

'I know, that's why I'm wearing a frock,' said the manager.

'I've nae money,' said McGonagall, feeling the manager's falsies.

'There's the bank interest,' said the manager.

'I'm not interested in banks,' said McGonagall.

A great groan came from the honeymoon room, followed by a thud.

'Oh,' said Rebecca. 'Have we got to do that?'

The honeymoon couple had now reached the head of the queue. Steam was issuing from the keyhole.

'Hurry up in there,' he said. 'Our best years are passing.'

'Ours have already gone,' said a weak voice from inside. A nightwatchman shone a torch.

'Can you put us up for the night?' said McGonagall.

'Yes,' said the nightwatchman. 'In the loft. Do you mind pigeons?'

'No,' said McGonagall. 'I'm not minding pigeons on ma wedding night.'

The happy couple spent their wedding night in the pigeon loft. About midnight a cross-eyed man came in through an attic window.

'Who are you?' said McGonagall.

'I'm Norris Drench, I'm a pigeon fancier.'

'Right,' said McGonagall. 'Take the pigeon you fancy and bugger off.'

A flurry of birdshit and feathers.

'It'll all be over soon,' said the pigeon fancier.

'I know, it's all over us,' said McGonagall. The nightwatchman came in with his torch.

'*Please* don't shine it *there*,' said McGonagall.

A policeman pushed his way through the crowd on the landing. 'Voilà le police,' he said.

'J'étais arrivé juste à temps,' McGonagall said.

'Nous avions visité la tour Eiffel l'été précédent.'

'Then,' said the policeman. 'You are in no condition to be doing that, and will you stop while I'm talking to you.'

A tall man with a whistle came in and blew it.

'Is it half-time then?' said McGonagall.

'No — it's full time. Leave the pitch,' said the man.

'Is that a badge you're wearing, or aren't you well?' said McGonagall.

'Have you stopped, darling?' said Rebecca underneath.

'Oh,' said the man. 'By the way, I'm from the Watch Committee.'

'Oh,' said McGonagall. 'What do you want?'

'I've come to watch,' he said. He then gave a blast on his whistle.

'Pourquoi,' said the policeman, 'are you blowing votre whistle?'

'Well,' said the blaster of the whistle, 'I am a honeymoon referee and I have to practise.' The policeman drew his truncheon and struck him in a sheltered area.

'You see, I am a policeman, and I have to practise too,' he said.

'Look,' said McGonagall pausing for breath. 'This is our honeymoon night. It's three in the morning and we haven't finished.' Watson in his nightgown pushed his way through the cheering crowd.

'Quiet, please, I am a doctor – I am this man's physician,' said Watson.

'And I am this man's referee,' said the referee.

'I must examine,' said Watson, 'the bride and groom to see if they are fit to carry on.' Watson threw back the bedclothes and waited for the steam to clear. He ran his stethoscope over the patients' nethers. A voice from down in the street came up.

'What about the bill from the YMCA?'

'I'll see you in the morning,' called McGonagall.

'Yes, but will I see you?' called the voice. Watson struck a dramatic pose.

'This honeymoon couple must stop! The groom has run out of it.'

'Give him an enema,' said the voice from the back.

'What good will it do?' said Watson.

'What harm will it do?' said the voice. A homing pigeon returned with a message strapped to its leg. It read: THE PRIME MINISTER OF ENGLAND IS STILL MISSING.

'Yes,' said McGonagall. 'For a start, he's missing all this.'

Watson struck a fresh pose. 'To avoid the message getting into enemy hands, I call for a volunteer to shoot the pigeon.'

The RSPCA man entered. 'I'm going to sue on behalf of the pigeon.'

THE COURT CASE
PART III

The famous Jamaican QC rose.

'Hello dere,' he said, and sat down.

'Is that all?' said the Judge.

'Dat am all,' said the QC.

'We're going to lose this case,' said Rebecca to McGonagall.

'He's a poor man's lawyer,' said McGonagall.

'We're not that poor,' said Rebecca.

The Judge spoke. 'Exactly who is the witness?'

'I am exactly who is the witness,' said the nightwatchman.

'Are you familiar with pigeons?' said the Judge.

'No sir,' said the witness. 'I'm a normal, happily married man.'

'He knows Mrs Gibbs,' shouted a voice.

'Will somebody explain who Mrs Gibbs is?' said the Judge.

'Your Honour, me ludd. You've heard of the Ancient Laye of Rome?'

'Yes,' said the Judge.

'Well, she's the one from Lewisham,' said QC Proles.

'I can't,' said the Judge, 'I can't see where Mrs Gibbs comes in.'

'She comes in round the back of the house at night,' said a voice.

'Who are you?' said the Judge.

'I'm an amnesiac,' said the voice.

'What is your name?' said the Judge.

'If only I knew,' wailed the voice.

'Now,' said the Judge. 'To be serious. Have the jury reached a decision?'

'Yes, we want to go home,' they said.

'Foreman of the jury,' said the Judge. 'The accused, how did you find him?'

'We found him in the WC.'

The clerk whispered to McGonagall. 'Excuse me, sir,' he said. 'There's a gypsy waiting for you outside.'

'Och, tell him I'll nae be long,' said McGonagall.

'He couldn't wait, sir,' said the clerk. 'He's thrown it over someone else.'

'Och, you can't rely on anyone,' said McGonagall.

Somewhere a dog barked.

'I'll get him,' thought McGonagall.

'Fred,' said another voice.

'What about Fred?' said the Judge.

'I've just remembered, that's who I am,' said the amnesiac.

'Fred who?' said the Judge.

'Fred Gibbs,' said the voice.

'Ah,' said the Judge. 'You must be married to that woman who goes in round the back. Are you separated?'

'No, I'm all in one piece,' said Fred.

'Are you living apart?' said the Judge.

'No, I'm on my own,' said Fred.

'Is she on her own?' said the Judge.

'No, she's living apart,' said Fred.

'The next witness,' said the clerk. 'The owner of the pigeons, nightwatchman John Grin.'

'Ah now,' said the Judge. Have you won any prizes with your pigeons?'

'Yes, m'lud, for the best pigeon pie at the Neasden Cooking Festival.'

Up stood the Jamaican QC.

'My client Mr McGonagall is innocent.'

'Rubbish,' said Fred Gibbs. 'My wife's been round the back of his house so many times he had the door taken off.'

''Tis a lie,' said McGonagall. 'I only had the cat flap enlarged.'

'Will you swear that?' said the Judge.

140

'Yes,' said McGonagall. 'I only had the bloody cat flap bloody well enlarged. Your honour,' said McGonagall. 'There's something I want to say.'

'Very well,' said the Judge.

'There's many a mickle makes a muckle,' said McGonagall.

'What was that?' said the Judge.

'It was something I wanted to say,' said McGonagall.

'Who shot the pigeon? Is something I wanted to say,' said the Judge.

'I did,' said Tom Drench, a noted pigeon assassin.

'Mr Drench, *you* had a gun on the night of the honeymoon. Do you normally carry a gun?'

'Yes,' said Drench. 'I carry it quite normally. Why?'

'Have you a licence?' said the Judge. 'Let me see it. This is a dog licence,' he said.

'Oh,' said Drench. 'Well, I normally carry a dog, as well.'

'I can't see how having a dog licence gives you the right to carry a gun,' said the Judge.

'Neither can I,' said Drench. 'But there you go.'

'You're accused of murdering a carrier pigeon,' said the Judge.

'Am I?' said Drench. 'Wait till I tell the boys back at the pub.'

'I can't wait for you to tell the boys back at the pub,' said the Judge.

'What about the hole in my pigeon loft?' said the nightwatchman.

'Oh,' said the Judge. 'What about the hole in it?'

'Well,' said the nightwatchman. 'I think he should pay for it.'

'You don't pay for holes,' said the Judge. 'If people went around paying for holes, I mean, they'd be selling holes in the shops.'

Proles QC stood up. 'My client would like to settle out of court.'

'Nonsense,' said the jolly Judge. 'It's raining out there, it's bad enough having it in here.'

'He and his wife would like to settle on the Costa Brava,' said Proles QC. 'My clients are very distressed over the loss of their pigeon, they wish to forget, and move to Spain.'

'You don't have to go to Spain to forget about pigeons. Where do you live?'

'In Neasden.'

'There,' said the Judge. 'You can forget about them in Neasden.'

Proles QC arose. 'My clients are going to Spain to forget Neasden as well.'

The Judge turned to McGonagall and Rebecca.

'How do you plead?'

McGonagall and his one-legged wife knelt down and burst into tears. Then McGonagall stood up. 'That's how we plead.'

The referee arose. 'Nobody has called me,' he said.

'Well, I'm calling you a silly bastard,' said McGonagall.

'Has this silly bastard got a previous record?' asked the Judge.

'Yes,' said the clerk. 'There is a cassette of him singing "Ave Maria" as a child.'

'"Ave Maria" as a child?' said the Judge. 'How old is she now?'

Proles QC stood up. 'Ave Maria's been dead 2,000 years. That's why she's not in court.'

In the distance a dog barked. 'I'll get him,' thought McGonagall.

McGonagall turned to his one-legged bride. 'I should have got Legal Aid,' he said.

'Listen,' said Rebecca. 'You couldn't even get lemonade.'

'Stop all this alternative comedy,' said the Judge. 'I will not have it in the court.'

'Then where would you like it?' said McGonagall. Proles QC stood up and pushed them back in.

'We have this *Jewish Chronicle* photo taken showing the dead pigeon.' The clerk of the Court passed it up to the Judge.

'Oh dear, I wish I had my grand piano here,' said the Judge.

'Why?' said the clerk.

'Because my reading glasses are on top of it,' said the Judge.

'Oh, don't worry,' said the clerk. 'You can borrow mine.'

'Where are they?' said the Judge.

'They're on top of my piano,' said the clerk.

'Oh dear,' said the Judge. 'Never mind, I'll use mine.'

'This photo is nothing to do with pigeon cruelty, this is an Arab hitting a donkey in Egypt.'

'Yes, m'lud,' said Proles. 'But that's the nearest we could get.'

'It's very unsatisfactory,' said the Judge. 'Mr Nightwatchman, stop doing that, please,' the Judge continued. 'Now, did any of your pigeons go in for racing?'

'Yes,' said the nightwatchman. 'One won the Derby.'

'That's a horse race.'

'I know,' said the nightwatchman. 'That's why he was disqualified.'

'Please,' said the Judge. 'Don't do that.'

'I can't help it, your honour,' said the nightwatchman. 'When my right hand gets cold, I plunge it deep into my pocket and play with my loose change.'

'What about your left hand?' said the Judge.

'I plunge that into boiling water,' said the nightwatchman.

'Doesn't that scald you?' said the Judge.

'No, I only have the boiling water lukewarm.'

'Then I'm in trouble and I have to manipulate the swonnicles.'

Suddenly the Jamaican QC did a rap dance.

'Highly irregular,' said the jolly Judge.

'Haile Selassie,' said the Jamaican QC.

'I'll have you for contempt,' said the Judge.

'I'll hab you for lunch,' said the Rasta QC.

'Now,' said the Judge. 'Are there any previous charges against McGonagall?'

'Yes,' said Proles QC. 'In World War Two he was charged by the 10th Panzer Division.'

'Was he with General Montgomery?' said the Judge.

'No, he was with General Electric,' said Proles.

'Objection,' said the Jamaican QC.

'Do you disagree?' said the Judge.

'No, I just object,' said the Jamaican QC.

'When did you take silk?' said the Judge.

'I never took silk, I took steroids.'

'Mr McGrinigal,' said the Judge. 'In the war, were you decorated?'

'Yes,' said McGrinigal. 'I've had "Doris, I love you" on my right arm.'

'I see,' said the Judge and summed up. 'I find William Topaz McGonagall not guilty of speeding, or the 800 unsolved murders on Scotland Yard's books. Case dismissed.'

McGONAGALL
GOES BIG TIME

McGonagall went to see his agent, Terence Blatt. Blatt shook his head.

'How do you feel about commercials?'

'I don't know, I've never felt one,' said McGonagall.

'Well,' said Blatt. 'One of the Brooke Bond monkeys has died.'

'He must ha' drunk the tea,' said McGonagall.

'They want someone to take his place.'

'Do I have to wear a monkey skin?' said Watson.

'I'm afraid, yes,' said Blatt.

'If I'm playing a monkey, the money's got to be right,' said McGonagall.

'It'll be in the neighbourhood of fifty pounds,' said Blatt.

'I don't like that neighbourhood,' said Watson.

'Look, no one will recognise you in a monkey skin,' said Blatt.

'Nobody recognises me in mine,' said McGonagall.

'Will you do it?' said Blatt. 'It could be your big chance, it could lead to other parts, like Bombay or Rangoon.'

McGonagall and Watson sat in the audition room, McGonagall in his monkey skin.

'Next please,' said the man. The director, Von Bulow, said, 'Hello, Mr McGonagall, you look splendid. Remember the other two chimps are real. Now you vill be at zer chimps tea party, ya?'

McGonagall took his place at the table.

'Right, action!' shouted Von Bulow.

'To be or not to be, that is the question,' said McGonagall.
'Cut, cut,' stormed Von Bulow. 'Vot are you doink?'
'Listen, I am an actor,' said McGonagall.
'You are supposed to make like a monkey, now try again. Action!' With that the large male chimpanzee brought the tea pot crashing down on McGonagall's head.
'Oh, my fucking head,' he wailed.
'Cut. Someone get rid of zat idiot,' shouted Von Bulow. Another chapter had closed.

> Ooooohhhhhh terrible Brooke Bond chimpanzee
> There were other monkeys to hit but he hit me
> Can't they see what a great actor I could be
> By letting me say to be or not to be?
> Try saying that in a monkey skin
> You realise that you can't win,
> It would have been worse luck
> If I'd had to play a duck.
> Still if it means a comeback
> I don't mind going quack quack.

'I'm sorry, Mr Von Bulow,' said McGonagall. 'I was put up to it.'
'Whoever put you up to it was an idiot,' said Von Bulow.
'You don't recognise great acting! See this,' McGonagall struck a pose. 'To be or not to be. There, don't tell me that's not great acting.' So Von Bulow didn't tell him.
'You'll be sorry,' said McGonagall, sweeping out the room into the cupboard. That night they found lodgings at Mrs Jones.
'It's only B and B, breakfast and bugger off.'
'What's fer breakfast?' said McGonagall, doing a little twirl on his toe.
'Rissoles,' she said. 'If you're late, the dog gets it.'

146

'No need for the dog to get it, we'll get it ourselves,' said Watson.

'Have you any form of identification?' she said.

'Yes,' said McGonagall. 'I'm William McGonagall and he's Doctor Watson.'

'Have you no papers?'

'No,' said McGonagall. 'But I can run out and buy some.'

'That's no bloody good,' she said. 'I mean identification papers.'

McGonagall and Watson both wrote their names on a piece of paper.

'There, that's who we are,' they said. She showed them their rooms.

'Have you got a shower?' said Dr Watson.

'Yes,' she laughed. 'And they all live here.' Her hollow silvery laughter rang down the hall.

'Now we're alone,' said McGonagall, 'we must press on with the search for the missing Prime Minister.'

'I personally am not missing him at all,' said Watson.

'They say,' said McGonagall, dusting his wallet, 'there's a reward out.'

'Out where?' said the snuff.

'Don't confuse me,' said McGonagall, ironing a pound note. Both men slept soundly. Watson sounded as though he was gargling with a raw egg.

'You asleep, Watson?' said McGonagall.

'Of course I am,' said Watson. 'You don't think I make this noise when I'm awake, do you?'

Still using the Burmese mangle as a front, McGonagall and Watson continued their search.

'Washing mangled while you wait,' said Dr Watson, taking snuff.

'Makers of snuff could be accused of stuffing their business up other people's noses,' he said.

147

All day they laboured, and not one single missing Prime Minister came by. McGonagall was losing heart and a lot of liquid.

'He must be somewhere,' said Watson.

'Yes, somewhere, that's where we should look.' They hailed a taxi.

'Take us somewhere,' said McGonagall, as it was his turn.

'Somewhere,' said the driver. 'Any special part?'

'Yes,' said McGonagall. 'Any special part.' He took them and their mangle to Eastbourne, the world's only above-ground cemetery. They didn't bury their dead, they recycled them. There were two on police duty. A small bald man with acne came by.

'I'll give you a pound for the mangle,' he said. He gave them a pound and they mangled it.

'No, I want to buy it,' he said.

'It'll cost you an arm and a leg,' said McGonagall starting to saw them off.

'No, no,' said Watson, for it was his turn. 'We want an arm and a leg in *money*.' That drove the man off.

'You'll pay for this,' he shouted, as he hopped off on one leg.

'No, we're doing it for free,' said McGonagall, as the last brick struck him.

''Ello, 'ello, 'ello,' said one policeman three times, or three policemen once. 'That is GBH,' he or three policemen said.

'What's GBH?' said Dr Watson, filling his pipe with shag.

'That was a case of GBHing if ever I saw one,' said the one or three police. 'I'll let you off with a warning. Gales force ten, Rockall, Fastnet, Irish Sea.'

'Thank you, officer,' said Watson. 'You're a fine-looking man, all three of you.' A charabanc of Japanese tourists dropped by.

'Harrow,' said the guide.

148

'This isn't Harrow,' said McGonagall. 'This is Eastbourne. Can't you see the dead?'

'What you do with mangle san?' said the guide.

'This is old-fashioned English piano,' said McGonagall, feeling a sale was nigh. He felt the guide.

'Please, can we hear piano.'

McGonagall turned the handle and sang, 'When it's midnight in Italy it's Wednesday over here'. The Japanese were ecstatic.

'Ah so, this good for karioke sing-song,' said head of the group, turning the handle and singing 'Misty'. 'Rook at me, I'm as ronery as a klitten up a tlee.'

'You're a fine singer, and that mangle is yours for five pounds.'

'Flive pounds, ah so it are bargain, ah so.'

'Ah so to you,' said McGonagall.

Straining in Japanese, they lifted the mangle aboard the charabanc. As they drove away, McGonagall could hear them singing 'The hills are arrive wiv the sound of music'.

IRISH GUARDS
TRY STRAINING*

'It's time for the Tug o'War,' said Mrs Whitehouse, holding up a referee.

'Take the strain,' said the referee. Both sides took the strain. 'Heave'. The Irish Guards team heaved and pulled McGonagall's team out the ground, across the road, up the

* See lumps in groin

street. They had to pause at the traffic lights, then the Irish Guards pulled their opponents up Whitehall across Horse Guards Parade, finally reaching Buckingham Palace. The Guards were declared the winners, with McGonagall's team second. The End.

THE CORPSE SINGS
AT MIDNIGHT

'Let's gae back to the office and see what's what,' said McGonagall.

'Yes,' said What's what Watson. 'What time does your watch say?'

'It doesn't say anything,' said McGonagall. 'I have to act as spokesman for it. It's eighteen hundred hours.'

'Blast,' said what's on Watson. 'My watch only goes up to twelve.'

At the office all hell had been let loose.

'Who let all hell loose?' said McGonagall.

'It was loose in here when I came in this morning,' said someone else.

'Well, let me get all hell let loose out the back window,' said McGonagall. They soon had all hell let loose out the back window. The man in the garden below came out and said, 'Who let all hell loose in my garden?' A policeman and an old Italian came in. He pointed at McGonagall.

'Dat's a-da man.'

'Sir, you are the dat's a-daman?' repeated the policeman.

'I am the dats a-daman?' said McGonagall. The policeman did a twirl with his truncheon.

'That's very clever, truncheon-twirling constable,' said What's what Watson.

'I do it mostly in private for the amusement of the inspector who lives a very boring life.'

'Hello, calling PC49,' said his police radio.

'Yes?' said PC49.

'I've just had a report that you've been twirling your truncheon in public,' said a voice. The constable gulped, a little lump went up and down his throat then came to a halt.

'It's my inspector,' he gibbered. 'What shall I say?'

'Here,' said McGonagall, taking the radio. 'Hello inspector, my name is dat's a-daman McGonagall,' said McGonagall.

'I'm very pleased to meet you,' said the inspector.

'Let me assure you that, although your policeman has twirled his truncheon, it has been done with great discretion.' The policeman whispered to McGonagall, 'Don't tell him I done it in front of an Italian.'

McGonagall spoke, 'Hello, Inspector, I want you to know that your constabule didn't twirl in front of an Italian.'

'That's very comforting news, Mr McGonagall. Can you hand me back to the constabule, I wish to comfort him over my suspicions.'

Meekly the policeman took the radio. 'Hello Inspector sir, it's me, Constable Drickle, known to you as PC49.'

'Listen, Drickle,' said the inspector.

Constabule Drickle listened. 'Hello, Inspector,' said Drickle. 'Are you hanging up?'

'No,' said the inspector. 'I'm leaning on the wall.'

'I wish you luck with it,' said Drickle. 'Over and out.' Constable Drickle gave a sigh of relief. 'Now to this case. This Italian said in the last war you shot his uncle, you shot an uncle in the Dolomites.'

McGonagall recoiled, 'I am innocent, I don't even know where your uncle's dolomites are.'

'Oh,' said Drickle. 'Not my uncle, he is the uncle.'

'I've never seen that uncle in my life. Where are his dolomites?' said McGonagall, red with anger, purple with rage and white with fury.

Constabule Drickle told the Italian, 'You are mistaken, this man says he does not know where your dolomites are.' Here he gave a furtive truncheon twirl.

'You won't tell the Inspector, will you?' he said to McGonagall.

'Don't worry, your truncheon twirl is safe with us.'

Sir Lew Grade came in.

'I'm making a picture called *The Corpse Sings at Midnight*,' he said. Was this McGonagall's big chance?

'Och, Sir Lew, that's great news.' Here he paused to prostrate himself before the movie mogul and place his foot on his head.

'Come in and have a chair.'

'No thanks,' said Sir Lew. 'I had one just before I came out. Now, how would you like to play the corpse?'

'Lying down,' said McGonagall.

'You sound like the right type for me,' said Sir Lew.

'Aye, see,' grovelled McGonagall from the flae. 'I'm already training for the part, and Sir Lew, if you want to wipe your shoes, just wipe them on me.' Lew dashed his cigar ash into McGonagall's face.

'Now this corpse has to sing, can you sing?'

'Can I sing?' said McGonagall, clearing his throat all over him. In a fine voice he sang:

> My Love is like a red red rose
> That blooms in early spring.

'Never mind,' said Sir Lew. 'We'll dub a voice over you. Bing Crosby, that's who'll do the voice.'

Training as a singing corpse

'He's dead,' said Watson.

'I know,' said Sir Lew. 'But he'll do fine for me.'

'What's wrong with Mick Jagger?' said McGonagall.

'We don't know,' said Sir Lew. 'For years doctors have been trying to find out.'

'Why not,' said Dr Watson, bowing his head. 'Dame Vera Lynn?'

'What? And start another war?' said Sir Lew, covering McGonagall with cigar ash. 'Right,' he continued. 'You can get up now, the audition's over.'

'Yes, most of it's over me,' said McGonagall.

'Now, what do you want in the way of money?'

'We don't want anything in the way, we want a clear view of it,' said Watson stuffing his business up his nose.

'We want money up front,' said McWatson.

'Good, as long as you don't want it up the back,' said Sir Lew. 'What do you have in mind?'

In mind, McGonagall had ten thousand pounds; in the bank he had fuck all.

'I think,' said Dr Watson, 'we're looking at ten thousand pounds.'

'No, you're not,' said Sir Lew. 'You're looking at the wall.'

Suddenly McGonagall and Watson sprinted around the room at speed; it was an attempt at distraction. Sure enough, when they finished they were both totally distracted.

'What was all that about?' said Sir Lew, flicking ash in McGonagall's face.

'That was about three hundred yards,' said Dr Watson, fighting for breath. 'You could call us fitness freaks.' Sir Lew didn't exactly call them that, but what he called them had hair on. With a sad grimace, Sir Lew took out his cheque-book. With a moan and tears streaming down his cheeks, he opened it.

'McGonagall, you drive a hard bargain,' he said.

'Yes, I left it parked outside,' said McGonagall.

'Name your price,' said Sir Lew.

'Name my price Tom,' said McGonagall, stalling for time.

'What figure do you have in mind?' said Sir Lew.

'Dolly Parton,' said McGonagall.

'Listen,' said Sir Lew, flicking ash up Watson's nose. 'I'm a man of few words.'

'So am I,' said McGonagall. 'Fish, leather, nuance. And that's only three of them.'

'Stop all this crapology,' said Sir Lew angrily, flicking hot ash all over Constabule Drickle, who was now handcuffed to the Italian uncle who was sitting on his lap.

'May I interrupt?' said Drickle.

'What do you mean, may you interrupt? You have,' said Sir Lew, red in the face and right knee.

154

'Mr McGonagall, I must ask you for a statement re the Italian uncle,' said the constabule.

'I swear,' said McGonagall in a flurry of cigar ash, 'I swear on this copy of Pirelli nudes, that I have never shot an Italian uncle, the nearest I got was a nephew.'

'Very well, I must ask you to attend Marylebone Crown Court to attend the brigglethuds,' said Drickle.

'Brigglethuds, what are they?' said Dr Watson.

'Don't ask me sir,' said Drickle. 'I'm not writing this book.'

A gamekeeper with a large red nose came in via the rope ladder to the window.

'Excuse me,' he said. 'I've been following a partridge and it flew in here.'

'There must be some mistake,' said Dr Watson through his nose. 'This has always been a partridge-free area.'

'Well,' said the gamekeeper. 'It definitely flew in here, so do you mind if I wait till it breaks cover?'

'That would be fine as long as it doesn't break anything else. I mean we have some fine Spode figures in here, in fact I'm one of them,' said Watson piffing at his pipe, or rather piping at his piff, or rather puffing at his piff and piping up his snuff, all of that. Sir Lew lit another three cigars.

'This *Corpse Sings at Midnight* film, do you realise it could make you Corpse of the Year? Three people already committed suicide to get the part. McGonagallstein, you are lucky to be alive to play it.' Constable Drickle raised his helmet and a partridge flew out. BANG BANG, that is, there should have been two bangs from the gamekeeper, but there weren't.

'I must have dozed off,' he apologised.

'What were you doing with a partridge up your helmet?' said Watson.

'He shoota ma uncle in da Dolomites,' said the Italian.

'McGonagall, here's my offer for playing the corpse, ten

pounds a day,' said Sir Lew. McGonagall fainted.

'It's the shock of money,' explained Watson.

'Look,' said Sir Lew. 'This film has got big parts.'

'So has McGonagall,' said Watson. On the flae McGona-gall groaned. A gypsy threw a bucket of water over him. McGonagall leapt to his feet with a 'Hey Ho Hup la, I didn't know they had showers here.'

'What about up-front money?' said Watson. Sir Lew took a handful of five-pound notes and stuffed them up Watson's front. While he was up there, he found a partridge.

'How did it get up there?' said the gamekeeper.

'A trick of the light,' said Watson.

'I,' said Sir Lew and his nose, 'will see you on the set.'

'Are you going?' said Wee Willy McGonagall.

'Just,' said Sir Lew, and left and right, and left and right, left, right, left, right, out of the room. McGonagall was moved to poem:

> Ooooooooooooo wonderful Sir Lew and his cigar
> He is going to make a star
> As a corpse on screen or stage.
> I'll be all the rage
> And people like Kylie Minogue
> Will say, 'Who is this new rogue.'

'Come on,' said the constabule to the Italian uncle. 'I'm taking you to the station.'

'I don't-a wanta catch-a-train,' said Italian uncle.

'You're not,' said the constabule. 'You're going to catch a police cell.'

THE MEDICAL
(FOR THE FILM)

'How do I stand, Doc?' said McGonagall.

'By standing up,' said the doctor.

'I'm not bad for fifty-eight.'

'You do mean 1958,' said the doctor. 'Touch your toes,' he added.

'It's no good, I cannae, it's hell doon there.'

'Yes, I suppose so,' said the doc. 'It's hell from here. How's your hearing?'

'Pardon?' said McGonagall.

'Now take a deep breath.' It only took McGonagall a few moments to regain consciousness.

'Where am I?' he said.

'Scotland,' said the doctor. 'Now I'm going to take a sample of your blood. Just a little prick.'

'I know you are,' said McGonagall.

'Will you be much longer?' said Watson.

'No, I've been five foot ten since I was twenty-one. If you want me longer than that, I can stand on a box.'

'Now, your eyes, read that wall chart,' said the doctor.

'What wall?' said McGonagall.

'You need glasses,' said the doctor.

'Rubbish, there's nae a thang wrong with my eyes,' said McGonagall.

'You're talking to the hatstand,' said the doctor.

'Och, it's just a wee joke,' said McGonagall.

'Talking of wee, I'll need a specimen. Can you fill that jar on the mantelpiece?' said the doctor.

157

'What, from here?' Silly McGonagall.

'Do you drink whisky?' asked the doctor, examining the specimen.

'Yes,' said McGonagall. 'Why?'

'Well, it's all in here,' said the doctor.

'Look, Doc,' said McGonagall. 'I'm entering for the Highland Games; with my physique, what do you think I should enter as?'

'Spectator,' said the doctor.

'I've never had any complaints so far,' said McGonagall.

'Well, you have now, you've got measles,' said the doctor.

'He'll be easily spotted,' said Dr Watson, who enjoyed a joke.

'That's the end of my examination,' said the doctor. 'That will be ten pounds.'

'Ten pounds?' he repeated. He forced open his wallet and over the next hour dragged ten pounds out, the tears streaming down his face. Part of the time he was given painkillers.

'No no,' said Dr Watson. 'He's too young to die.'

'Nonsense, he's just the right age,' said the doctor, drying the notes by the fire.

THE HIGHLAND GAMES,
AW AND AW

The officials saw McGonagall and relegated him to the caber tossing for over-sixties.

'But I'm only fifty,' he complained.

'Don't worry,' said the official. 'By the time the games finish you'll be sixty.' He was put in the rare category.

'Now,' said the loudspeakers. 'A special lone event for contestants with measles — William Topaz McGonagall, aged fifty.'

McGonagall saw the caber.

'Take the strain,' said the umpires. Two giant Scots held up the caber for McGonagall.

'OK, I've got it,' he strained. There he stood with the fifteen-foot caber, the sweat pouring from every pore and orifice. The going underfoot was soft; gradually the straining Scot sank into the mud, then with a tremendous heave his kilt ripped at the waist, revealing a cock o' the North.

'Och, it's nae gude, I canna toss the caber.' He was pulled from his hole and laid on the flae where he started to sink again. Dr Watson came to his assistance.

'You're a gude friend,' said the measled Scot.

'Ladies and gentlemen,' rang out the announcement, 'Mr William McGonagall has retired from the fifty-year-old with measles event.'

Suddenly on the end of a whisky bottle appeared a shit-covered Scot.

'Och, it's ma fither,' said McGonagall in despair. 'Wait till Mother sees you, she'll give you what-for.' Sure enough, his mother came along and gave McGonagall's father a what-for. They took it home by the fire. There was McGonagall's aged grandfather and incontinent grandmother in a pool around her feet.

'She's leaking,' said McGonagall. 'Call a plumber.' It was no surprise when a Red Indian with a sink pump arrived.

'Me Chief Call-out-Fee-Twenty-five-pounds.'

'Have ye got blood pressure?' said McGonagall.

'No, me got tyre pressure 28 front, 24 back.'

'My grandmother's leaking, can you stop it?' said McGonagall.

'No, me not stop it,' said the chief. 'She should stop it then I can go home with call-out fee.'

'Look here, Clever Dick . . .'

'No, me no got clever Dick, just ordinary hang-down one,' said the chief.

'Och,' said McGonagall. 'You may have a call-out fee, but you won't hear me calling it out.' Dr Watson looked up the word Incontinent in the medical dictionary and came up with a cure.

'It's a bucket,' he said. McGonagall's father started up on the bagpipes. Outside the charabanc of Japanese tourists arrived.

'We come see melly Scrotland,' said one. 'Please Schottlish man, we want photograph,' said another.

'I'm solly,' said McGonagall. 'I haven't got a photograph, will an old Scottish bucket do?'

'Oh boy,' said one. 'Yes, we take Schottlish brucket.'

'Gude, you can empty it outside,' said McGonagall. 'Look, I'll show you how.' McGonagall emptied it over a sleeping gypsy who leapt to his feet with a 'Hi Ho Hup La, I didn't know there was a public convenience here.' A taxi pulled up, out stepped a one-legged woman.

'It's the wife,' said McGonagall. 'Welcome to Scotland.'

'You're welcome to it,' said Rebecca. 'Where are the fish knives?'

For the benefit of the reader, the fish knives were in Arabia at a picnic thrown by the Aga Khan. He had thrown it fifty yards and the diners had to run for it.

The piper was now playing 'Knees Up Mother Brown'.

'Here, Rebecca,' said the prancing McGonagall. 'Do the knee up with me.'

'Oh no,' she said. 'I've only got one knee and, when that's up, there's nothing underneath.'

'Come on you,' said the prancing McGonagall to the coach party, 'clap hands.'

'Ah yes, crap hands,' they said. It was getting hot in the room. McGonagall went outside for a breather. A gypsy threw a bucket of water over him. In the distance, a dog barked. 'I'll get him,' thought McGonagall. The coach party all came out and one said, 'Prease tell us, is anything worn under the kilt?' In one flash McGonagall revealed all to the people of Nippon.

'Roch Ness monster,' they said as the cameras flashed.

OOOHHHH TERRIBLE NIGHT OF THE KILT AND THE FEATHER

Back at the office, a Police Inspector and a constabule were waiting.

'Mr McGonagall, I have a warrant for your arrest.'

'Och,' said McGonagall. 'That's for my arrest, anything for me?'

'What's the charge?' said Watson. The constabule drew out a bugle and sounded the charge.

'It sounds serious,' said McGonagall, with a wink and a tap on the nose.

'Indecent exposure,' said the inspector. 'Distressing Japanese tourists.'

'Listen,' said McGonagall. 'Japanese tourists are bloody distressing.'

'I must warn you anything you say will be taken down,' said the inspector.

'I can see this coming,' said Dr Watson.

'Trousers,' said McGonagall. It all looked grim. If McGonagall lost this case, the name of McGonagall would be McGonagall.

> Oooohhh terrible night of the kilt,
> Which did for to make the Nips all wilt.
> It was only a brief flash of ma willy,
> Something I thought was just silly.
> It was nothing special to see,
> Except it was inches thirty-three.

When the Nips all saw it appear,
They did for to clap and cheer.
Mind you I've had the clap before,
Which I had caught in Singapore.
Now I've got to go to court,
All because of a bit of sport.

Before the court case, Rebecca wanted to finish the honeymoon.

'Well, you'll have to finish it on your own,' said McGonagall. 'I'm busy training to be a convict.'

'You silly Scotsman,' said Dr Watson. 'You won't be convicted, it'll only be a fine.'

'It'll only be a fine what?' said McGonagall. The nude banjo player came out of the cupboard and plucked 'Ole Man River'.

'It's to welcome you back home,' he said.

'I'm not back home,' said McGonagall, 'I'm here.' Watson stood and scratched them. He drew on his pipe, he drew on the walls and he drew on his experience.

'You'll need a good liar,' he said.

'You mean lawyer,' said McGonagall.

'You mean bastard,' said Dr Watson. Sir Lew returned in a cloud of money. He saw one-legged Rebecca. 'My life, *she's* what I need for the film. Come dear, the Rolls is outside.'

'Don't listen to him,' said McGonagall. 'We've got rolls in the breadbin.'

Sir Lew smirked. He liked a good smirk.

'Listen, your leg will be the talk of London.' With no more ado he took her away.

'See that?' said McGonagall. 'When he left, he had no more ado, he must have used it all up on the way here.'

A plumber arrived. 'I've come to fix your leaky tap,' he said.

'We haven't got a leaky tap,' said Watson.

'I know,' said the plumber. 'I've come to give you one.'

'Bugger off,' said McGonagall, rising.

'Oh,' said the plumber. 'Don't be like that.'

'Don't be like what?' said McGonagall, rising.

'Like 'er,' the plumber pointed to a wastepaper basket. 'Like that.'

'Bugger off,' said McGonagall, rising. The plumber burst into tears.

'Here,' said McGonagall, rising. 'You're leaking, you need a plumber.'

'Don't,' said the plumber. 'I'm not really a plumber. I'm an unemployed mind-reader looking for work.'

'OK,' said McGonagall, rising. 'Read my mind.'

'I'll have to concentrate.' The mind-reading plumber closed his eyes and placed his hands on McGonagall's head.

'Oh,' he said in a strange whining voice. 'I can see you are going to pay me a hundred pounds for reading your mind.'

McGonagall stepped back with a laugh, and fell out of the window.

'Someone is going to say "Oh I think I've broken my fucking leg",' said the mind-reader.

From below came the voice of someone saying, 'Oh I think I've broken my fucking leg.' It wasn't McGonagall, but someone he'd fallen on.

'No wonder you're out of work,' said Watson to the mind-reading plumber.

Who had McGonagall fallen on?

'My name is Tom Hard-Times.' So, dear reader, McGonagall had fallen on hard times. Now read on.

'Thank you for breaking my fall,' said McGonagall to Tom Hard-Times. 'Do you often groan on the pavement?'

'No, this is my first time,' said Hard-Times. An ambulance

164

pulled up. Out came two men with a stretcher. 'Did you see the accident?' they said.

'See it? I was it,' said Hard-Times.

A policeman came and blew his whistle. 'What has happened?' he said.

'I'll tell you,' said McGonagall. 'A policeman has just come up and blown a whistle.'

'Sir, did you collide with this pedestrian?' said the police.

'Yes,' said McGonagall.

'What speed were you doing?' said the police.

'I'd say forty miles an hour,' said McGonagall.

'You'd say that?' said the police. 'What were you travelling in?'

'A kilt,' said McGonagall.

'Is that a make of car?' said the police.

'No, it's a make of kilt.'

'Can I see your licence?' said the police. With a flourish and a graceful pirouette, McGonagall handed it across.

'This is a dog licence,' said the police.

'Bow wow wow,' said McGonagall.

'Yes sir,' said the police. 'This licence appears to be in order.'

The policeman turned to Mr H. Times. 'Do you wish to make a statement, sir?'

'Yes,' said Mr H. Times. 'Oh, I think I've broken my fucking leg.'

'Could you not say fucking, sir,' said the police.

'Very well, Oh fuck, I think I've broken my leg,' said Hard-Times.

'That won't sound good in court,' said the police.

'Well, don't say it in court, say it in a barrack room,' said Hard-Times. The policeman took off his helmet, took up a dramatic pose and sang 'A Policeman's Life is not a Happy One'. Singing and smiling and deranged, he wandered down the street and out of sight. They never saw him again. Dr Watson arrived.

'I've just had a telephone call saying the missing Prime Minister is being held prisoner in Blackpool.'

'Blackpool?' said McGonagall in horror, 'Och, I wish I had some mustard,' he said.

'Why?' said Watson 'I like mustard. It would help jolly up our stay in Blackpool.'

'I've had quite a few stays in Blackpool, most of them off landladies. I had to settle the rent in several ways, the last time was standing in a coal bucket. It was over her head and me hanging on the handle.'

'We *must* make some money,' said Watson.

'I *was*, but the machine broke down,' said McGonagall.

'Oh dear,' said Watson ad-libbing.

'The machine got jammed,' said McGonagall.

'You were a fool to put jam in it,' said Watson. 'Didn't you have any three-in-one oil?'

'No, I only had three-in-one jam.'

'What coins were you turning out?' asked Watson.

'Strawberry-flavoured fifty pences,' said McGonagall. 'I had three in my sandwich for breakfast.'

'So you're going to be passing counterfeit coins are you?' said Watson. 'There's a message coming over the fax machine, it says "Happy Birthday to you".'

'It's nae ma birthday,' said McGonagall.

'No, it's the fax machine's birthday, it's six months old today.'

'No wonder we can't understand what it's saying,' said McGonagall.

'Every time it sends a message a wet nurse comes in.' A wet nurse came in.

'You're as dry as a bone,' said McGonagall.

'Yes, it's my day off,' said the wet nurse.

'It's time you had it off,' said McGonagall and pulled her into a cupboard.

'That's better,' he said, reappearing.

'You must read my book on how to get rid of wet nurses in three easy lessons, using only one cupboard and three-in-one jam,' said McGonagall.

'Did you pay her?' said Watson from on top of the cupboard.

'What are you doing on top of that cupboard?' said Miss Moneypenny.

'Believe it or not,' said Watson. 'I'm doing a Charleston with as little body movement as possible.'

The wet nurse came out. 'Any more of that going?' she said.

'All right,' said McGonagall, dragging her in. 'Just one for aul' lang syne.' He stepped in, gave her an auld lang syne and came out refreshed.

'Should auld acquaintance be forgot?' said the nurse, when she came out.

'Yes, they should, especially if I owe them money,' said McGonagall.

'Are you mean?' said the nurse.

'Yes. If I was a ghost I wouldn't even give you a fright,' said McGonagall. There was a thud and Watson fell off the cupboard.

'Ups a daisy,' said McGonagall.

'Oooooooo,' said Watson.

'You ungrateful swine,' said McGonagall. 'I give you a merry oops a daisy, and all you can do is groan.'

'Don't be too hard on him, he's only just reached the floor,' said Miss Moneypenny.

'This is going to put a great strain on our relationship,' said Watson.

'What is?' said McGonagall.

'This is,' said Watson, reaching up under his kilt and squeezing them.

'Here, here,' said McGonagall. 'Stop that. Don't you remember we agreed to stop all that after we left the monastery?'

'Wait,' said Miss Moneypenny. 'There's something coming through the fax machine.'

'It's orange juice,' said McGonagall.

'Mr McGonagall,' said Miss Moneypenny. 'Shouldn't you be doing something about the missing Prime Minister?'

'Yes, I'm going to drink this orange juice,' said McGonagall.

'I wonder where those fish knives are now?' said Watson in a dreamy faraway voice. If he but knew, the fish knives were three-quarters of a mile from the Aga Khan and extending their lead, but hotly pursued by Rebecca in her search for marital fulfilment.

'You're spoiling yourself for the part,' said Sir Lew, pursuing her on his stretched camel. 'Look, if you go on like this, you won't have a leg to stand on,' said Sir Lew, through his stretched cigar.

'Wait,' he said. 'Something's coming through my fax machine. It's McGonagall.'

'What are you doing to my wife and her leg?' said McGonagall.

'She's gone on ahead,' said Sir Lew.

'She's gone on her head?' said McGonagall. 'Och, she must be saving her leg for the finish.'

'I've had enough of this,' said McGonagall, he and Watson disappearing into the fax machine and reappearing on a coach travelling from Victoria.

'What do you want?' said the conductor.

'We want to know when the bus is going to start,' said McGonagall.

'It's not going to,' said the conductor. 'This is a bus for people who don't like going anywhere. And that'll be a pound.'

So they took the pavement back to the office. There was a knock at the door, it was them.

'Come in,' said McGonagall. Them came in.

'Who are you?' said Miss Moneypenny.

'We are them,' said them.

'Oh, it's them again,' said Miss Moneypenny. 'They were here this morning.'

The nude banjo player sprang fully plucked from the cupboard, dressed for Ascot.

'Ah, changed your mind, eh?' said McGonagall.

'Oh nudity is a thing of the past,' said the banjo player. 'I couldn't hold out any longer.'

'I've never seen you holding anything out,' said McGonagall.

'Can I borrow your pavement to get to Ascot?' said the banjo player.

'This pavement only goes to Neasden,' said McGonagall.

'Are there any races there?' said the banjo player.

'Ah yes, Jamaicans, English, Irish, Welsh and Pakistanis.'

'What time do they start?' said the banjo player.

'They started back in 1950,' said McGonagall. 'You'd better hurry up, they must be near the winning post.'

'Do you think I'll be in time to see them,' said the banjo player.

'You're too late,' said McGonagall. 'The result's just coming through on the fax – in the human race today, the Irish came last.'

'Good job I didn't bet on them,' said banjo. 'If I hurry I might be able to catch them together.'

'It's very painful when you catch them together,' said McGonagall.

'I caught my wife together once, and I've never forgiven her. Do you know what she said?' said Watson.

'No,' said the banjo player. 'I wasn't there.'

'Oh, what a pity,' said Watson. 'Now I'll never know.'

169

'Do what?' said Watson, sliding down files A-Z, and scorching them.

'Do you know the last thing I'd do?' said McGonagall.

'What?' said Watson.

'Die,' said McGonagall with a tap on the nose, a wink, a pirouette, painting the walls, greasing the car, mowing the lawn, varnishing the piano, and shouting 'Chestnuts, hot chestnuts, penny a bag! Tomatoes, lovely ripe tomatoes, cheese rolls, salami and day-old chicks'. Here was a man with a vision. He could be a Tesco, a Safeway or a Payless.

'I'll have a day-old chick,' said the banjo player.

'Sorry, we're out of those, I've got a day-old tomato.'

'Is it going cheap?' said the banjo.

'No,' said McGonagall. 'Only the chickens go cheep.'

In came the following: Sir Lew Grade and his psychiatrist, followed by Rebecca with a set of fish knives, her mother, her father and a French Catholic priest.

'A sight for sore eyes,' said McGonagall.

'What is?' said Watson.

'The Wapping Eye Hospital,' said McGonagall. 'Laugh please.'

'Never mind people with Wapping eyes,' said Sir Lew.

'Peace on you,' said the French priest.

'Don't you dare,' said McGonagall. 'This kilt has just come back from the cleaners.'

'I took him there,' said Watson.

'You took him to the cleaners?' said Sir Lew.

'Oh,' said Rebecca. 'My leg keeps giving way.'

'What is it, oncoming traffic?' said McGonagall.

'Oh don't make jokes,' she cried.

'You think that's funny,' said McGonagall. 'Wait till you hear the next line.'

'Peace on you,' said the French priest.

'Not again,' said McGonagall. 'We've only just cleared the last lot up.'

'I've no idea,' said Dr Watson. 'But nevertheless a bag of hot chestnuts for a penny would be good value for a drowning person.'

'Did I hear somebody selling chestnuts?' said the nude banjo player, coming out with a pluck.

'From what I can see of you, hot chestnuts are the last things you need,' said McGonagall.

'All right, I'll wait till then,' said banjo.

'Just knock when you're dying,' said McGonagall. 'And we'll throw them in.'

'I must say, there's been a lot of passing trade for a hot chestnut-seller on the shipping lanes,' said Miss Moneypenny. 'It's a wonder nobody's ever thought of it.'

'My father thought of it,' said McGonagall. 'But by the time he got there with his hot chestnuts, the ship had gone down.'

'Did he save any passengers?' said Miss Moneypenny.

'Yes, he saved a Miss Rita Thighs. He saved her for over three hours, before throwing her back in,' said McGonagall.

'That's a terrible thing to do,' said Miss Moneypenny.

'Yes,' said McGonagall. 'And to make matters worse, while he was doing it, his chestnuts went cold.'

'Were they frozen assets?' asked Miss Moneypenny.

'Yes, he had those as well,' said McGonagall.

'It's not much of a life on a filing-cabinet,' said Dr Watson. 'I don't see what people see in it.'

'Who put you up to it?' said McGonagall.

'Nobody,' said Watson. 'I got up here by myself, I'm full of confidence.'

'Have you ever thought of selling chestnuts up there?' said McGonagall.

'No, that's the last thing I'd do,' said Watson.

'You'd better hurry,' said McGonagall. 'That's what the banjo player's waiting to do.'

'How would you like to hear me play "Oh Dem Golden Slippers"?' said the banjo player.

'On the *Titanic*,' said McGonagall.

'I don't find that funny,' said the banjo.

'*You* don't find it funny,' said McGonagall. 'You should have heard what the passengers had to say.'

'What did they have to say?' said banjo.

'Help,' said McGonagall.

'I don't think that's very funny either,' said the banjo.

'I totally agree with you,' said McGonagall. 'I don't think saying "Help" is funny, but then what makes you think I'm trying to make you laugh, you miserable bastard?'

'I'll have you know,' said the banjo, 'that my parents were legally married.'

'That doesn't stop you from being a miserable bastard,' said McGonagall.

'I'm not staying here to be insulted by you or them.' And so saying, he stripped off his Ascots, and in his nude beauty he returned to the cupboard, to the life he yearned for and loved. Once inside he could be heard secretly tuning his banjo and reciting 'Lady Windermere's Fan'.

'I didn't know Lady Windermere had a fan, at least not a nude one,' said Watson.

'Oh yes, those are the kind they like best,' said McGonagall.

'Do you know,' said McGonagall, 'he's absolutely right. There's nothing funny about those passengers shouting help. What else do you say when you're drowning?'

'You can say hot chestnuts penny a bag,' said Watson.

'But that won't stop you from drowning,' said McGonagall.

'No, but they're very tasty,' said Watson.

'Where are you going to get a chestnut-seller on the *Titanic*?' said McGonagall.

'Oh, another joke,' said Rebecca.

'You should be on the stage.'

'The only stage that would take him,' said Groucho Marx, 'would be Wells Fargo.'

'How did *you* get in?' said McGonagall.

'It's a new device that lets you walk through walls, it's called a door,' said Groucho. 'And talking of walls, I notice this room has only got three. Aren't you cutting it fine?'

'Let me explain,' said Dr Watson from the top of the wardrobe.

'What's he doing up there?' said Groucho. 'Can't you afford a monkey?'

'You see,' said Dr Watson. 'We're getting our walls on the instalment system, and the fourth one is due any day.'

A free-standing Groucho Marx moustache

'Some of my best friends are Jews,' said Groucho.

'My life! It's Groucho Marxstein,' said Rebecca.

'That name rings a bell,' said Watson.

'You must think you're Quasimodo,' said Groucho Marxstein.

'What's going on here?' said the nude banjo player leaping from the cupboard.

'I've heard of hang-ups, but this is ridiculous,' said Groucho.

'I hang clothes up in my cupboard. Who does he think he is, a suit?'

'Oh blessings on you,' said the French priest. 'I am collecting for ze poor.'

'Shall we form a line?' said Groucho.

'Many poor people have no clothes.'

'Well, we've got one here,' said Groucho, eyeing the banjo player.

'Mr Marx,' said Watson. 'Where are your brothers?'

'They are at the race track, two of them are horses.'

'You're a fine-looking woman,' said Groucho. 'And she's doing it all with one leg. It takes me all my time with two. What's your secret?'

'Mr Marx,' said McGonagall coming back into the book. 'Have you got any Jewish blood?'

'Yes, I've got three bottles in the fridge. I'm expecting Dracula for dinner, who are you expecting?'

'I want you all to kneel down,' said the priest.

'You want me all to kneel down?' said Groucho. 'What about the rest of them?'

'You must not be disrespectful to a man of the cloth,' said the priest.

'My father's got three bales of cloth at home and I'm disrespectful to him and he's never complained.'

'You are a man of ze Jewish persuasion,' said the priest.

'I may be Jewish, but I don't need persuading,' said Groucho. 'Do you want to try?'

'You believe you are God's chosen people,' said the priest.

'Well, so far he hasn't chosen me,' said Groucho. 'Perhaps he's had enough.'

'I,' said Miss Moneypenny, 'find you a fascinating creature.'

'All right,' said Groucho. 'Let me know when you find it and we'll take it for a walk. I remember I once took a gander round the town and it did us both good. Have you got anything on tonight, Miss Moneypenny?' he asked.

174

'No,' she said.

'Then you're going to get cold,' said Groucho. 'I can arrange for the bed to be turned down.' On the spur of the moment, McGonagall poemed:

Ooooohhhhhh terrible Marx Brother,
Of which Groucho is another,
Always making wisecracks,
In front and sometimes behind other people's backs.
He smokes a big cigar,
Which must contain nicotine tar;
His motor coat has a very long tail,
And has nothing to do with the Tay whale.
And if you please,
He walks around town with bent knees,
He tries to win the affection of Miss Moneypenny,
But the trouble is she hasn't any.
That's all I have to say,
About Groucho Marx today.

'It'll never be a hit,' said Groucho.

'It's wonderful!' said Sir Lew. 'I'll have it set to music.'

'I'd have it set sail to Africa,' said Groucho.

'I've come over giddy,' said Watson.

'That's fine,' said Groucho. 'As long as you don't come over here.'

'Mr McGonagallstein,' said Sir Lew, 'your wife has failed me, the film has folded.'

'What about her leg?' said McGonagallstein.

'That's folded as well,' said Sir Lew. 'In the death scene, instead of sliding gracefully to the floor, her leg jack-knifed.'

'Couldn't she die standing up?' said McGonagall.

'I died standing up at the Met,' said Groucho. 'And I had two legs at the time. I remember it as though it was only yesterday. Come to think of it, it was yesterday.'

'Listen,' said Sir Lew, his voice choked with money.

'We've got to reinforce her leg.'

'Good,' said Groucho. 'Send for the Irish Guards, they're the best reinforcements around here.'

'There's nae need to go to extraordinary lengths,' said McGonagall.

'The most extraordinary length I ever went to was six foot nine,' said Groucho.

There came a wailing of bagpipes.

'Och, it's me fither,' said McGonagall.

'He's taking his time,' said Groucho.

'That's a change, he's usually doing it,' said McGonagall.

'Look,' said Sir Lew. 'About the way your wife's leg has been acting, I want to ask Mr Herpes here, the psychiatrist, for his advice.'

'In my opinion,' said the psychiatrist. 'It's all in the mind.'

'Her leg is all in the mind?' said McGonagall. 'I thought it was hanging down underneath?'

'Yes,' said the psychiatrist. 'It is hanging down underneath, but her mind has no confidence in it.'

'Her mind has no confidence in her leg?' said McGonagall.

'Every minute of this is costing me money,' said Sir Lew, sobbing on his accountant's shoulder. 'What her leg needs is a week in the South of France,' said the psychiatrist.

'A week in the South of France?' said McGonagall. 'It's weak enough over here.'

'All I know is,' said Rebecca. 'I saved the fish knives from Saddam Hussein.'

'Don't think I'm not grateful,' said McGonagall.

'All right,' said Rebecca. 'I won't think you're not grateful.'

'Can I get a line in here?' said Groucho. The nude banjo player leapt from the cupboard. Rebecca screamed, she'd never seen chestnuts like that before.

'I think I'm going to faint,' she said. 'Someone hold the fish knives.'

'Quick, put something under her,' said McGonagall.

'The broom handle,' said Groucho. Rebecca clutched it and slid gracefully to the floor.

'That's it,' said Sir Lew through his money. 'What we need for the ending is a broom handle. I'll have one made in gold lamé and pink tinsel with strobe lighting for the finale. And quick, sign up the nude banjo player and his hot chestnuts to help her faint on the night.'

'Most people faint on the carpet,' said Groucho.

'Let us thank God,' said the priest, 'for the success of this mission.'

'Not forgetting the NatWest and the Bradford and Bingley,' said Sir Lew, squeezing the tears out of his wallet.

Rebecca lay pale and still on the floor as McGonagall tried to force some brandy down his throat.

'She's starting to look much better,' said McGonagall.

'So are you,' said Groucho. Dr Watson clambered down to the unconscious Rebecca.

'This woman needs vitamins,' he said. 'A, E, B . . .'

'That's a funny way to spell vitamins.' The door opened and McGonagall's father burst in with a wail of bagpipes.

'My son, my son,' he said.

'Och, he thinks there's two of me,' said McGonagall.

'He must be drinking the same stuff,' said Groucho. Rebecca got to her foot.

'Are you feeling better?' said Dr Watson.

'Better schmetter, what's it matter, as long as you got your strength and health, oy vay, my Yiddisher mama . . .' said Rebecca. 'Help, here come the floor,' she said.

'Can you give absolution to a dying leg?' said McGonagall.

'Absolutely,' said the priest.

'All right, have it your way,' said McGonagall. 'Can you give absolutely to a dying leg?'

'Is it an emergency?' said the priest.

'No, it's a leg,' said McGonagall.

'Are you sure,' said ze priest.

'Absolutely,' said McGonagall.

'Absolution,' said the priest.

'Was that it?' said McGonagall, amazed at the speed of the ritual.

'Oui, oui, zat was ze new quick absolution for one-legged persons,' said the priest. 'There is a fee.'

'There is also a fie, foe and a fum,' said Groucho.

'Her pulse is back to normal,' said Dr Watson.

'That's more than you can say for the rest of her,' said Groucho.

'Perhaps you did not 'ear me?' said the priest. 'I said there is a fee.'

'As I said, there's also a fie, a foe and fum, for the second and last time,' said Groucho. 'Can anybody smell the blood of an Englishman, or is it just me?'

'This is costing me piles,' said Sir Lew.

'I had them once,' said McGonagall. 'They cost me a pretty penny.'

'This means the bottom has fallen out of the market,' said Groucho.

'Can you carry on, my dear?' said Sir Lew to Rebecca.

'She's been carrying on ever since I met her,' said McGonagall.

'Ah,' said Dr Watson through his stethoscope. 'The roses are coming back to her knee. She'll soon be back on her foot again.' McGonagall turned towards the priest and said, 'Thanks to vous, here's something towards the church,' and threw a brick at it.

'Un moment,' said le priest. 'I was looking for something in the way of money.'

'I see nothing in the way of money,' said McGonagall, 'except me. So I should be the first to see it.'

'Sacré bleu,' said the priest.

'Gott in Himmel,' said the psychiatrist.

'This girl is running a temperature,' said Dr Watson.

'That's nothing, her father's running a pawn shop,' said Groucho.

There was a great scream from McGonagall's father who was bent double.

'My God, he's caught them together,' said McGonagall. 'Ma mither must have starched his jockey pants.'

'I'd say,' said Dr Watson, 'he's played his last pibroch.' There was a low moan from Rebecca, a second scream from McGonagall's fither, a burst of song from a Black and White minstrel and the hiss of escaping steam from the wardrobe. None of these incidents made the headlines, but they all happened. And it was just a coincidence that a man was found dead in a matchbox at Charing Cross Station with the headline:

EARTHQUAKE AT CHARING CROSS STATION,
WORLD'S SMALLEST MAN KILLED BY
ESCAPING JET OF STEAM.

'One minute he was there, the next minute he was gone,' said the station porter.

THE DENOUEMENT,
PART III

'Listen everybody,' said Miss Moneypenny, 'and that includes me. We are supposed to be looking for the missing Prime Minister.'

'I've searched high and low for him,' said McGonagall.

'Perhaps he's somewhere in between,' said Miss Money-penny.

McGonagall ran to the far wall and back three times.

'Never do things by halves,' he said, then ran another three.

'If only your dear grandmother was alive to see you today,' said McGonagall's fither, bent double and clutching both of them

But, alas! McGonagall's grandmither was not alive today, so she wouldn't be seeing him. As a girl his grandmither was poverty-stricken and eked out a living by gathering lobsters in the heather. Having no knowledge of their real value, she sold them to passing tourists for a thousand pounds a claw. Such was the poverty in the land, for the want of money her Rolls Royce never left the garage. She died from a surfeit of Lampreys and on top of all that, she wouldn't be seeing McGonagall today.

'Ah, *c'est la vie*,' said le French priest.

'What is?' said le McGonagall.

'This is,' said the priest. 'It's God's will.'

'I didn't know he'd made one,' said McGonagall. 'Tell me, oh son of the cloth, what's life like without women?' said McGonagall.

'Sacré bleu,' said the priest. 'You see that tree over there?'

'Yes,' said McGonagall.

'Well, it's like that.'

'Do you dream about women?' said McGonagall.

'No,' said the priest, 'I dream about trees, but when I wake up in the morning they are gone.'

'Perhaps you should get up later,' said McGonagall.

'I do get up later,' said the priest. 'And this is it.'

'Tell me father, do you think priests should be allowed to marry?' said McGonagall.

'If they love each other,' said the priest.

'I married a vicar once,' said Miss Moneypenny. 'He was

180

so rarely in his cassock that people thought I had married a nudist. He started a nude church, but in cold weather the attendances dropped off. And that wasn't the only thing.'

There was a sudden burst of bagpipe playing from the fither.

'Och, he's OK, they must be hanging normally again,' said McGonagall.

'Just a minute,' said Sir Lew from somewhere in his wallet. 'Do you remember this?' Sir Lew took up a loan free pose and sang 'White Christmas'. 'That's a famous Berlin number.'

'Well, I don't care if it comes from Tokyo.'

'You and your clenched money are a pain in the arse,' said Fither.

'What?' said Sir Lew in a financial rage. 'I'm a self-made man.'

'Och', said the fither. 'I see you ran out of material.'

'That's nothing, this morning he ran out on his wife,' said Groucho.

'It was only a matter of a few shillings. My wife is a spendaholic,' said Sir Lew.

'If my wife went around spending holics, I'd leave her as well,' said Groucho. 'You're a man after my own heart, and I don't think my liver and lungs are safe either.' Rebecca gave a low moan. It was the first in a series of five.

'She must be getting better,' said Dr Watson. 'She managed them on her own. Up till now I've been having to do them for her. I come from a family of moaners. My father moaned at the funeral of King George V. He moaned at the death of Lord Kitchener, he moaned at ·the death of Mrs Simpson, and he moaned, privately, at the death of Lord Salisbury.'

'Are you sure he wasn't just a miserable bastard?' said McGonagall.

'Yes, he was that as well,' said the doctor. 'It got him a knighthood, and he used to wear it during the day as well. He was arrested for exposing himself to his wife.'

'That's not a crime,' said le French priest.

'It is in the middle of a Lord Mayor's banquet,' said Watson. 'He was stripped of his knighthood and so he had to wear a mac. He wandered the embankment, exposing himself at intervals. The best interval he did was during *Private Lives*. He went down better than the play and received many offers of marriage from ladies of rank.'

'If she was anything like his latest wife, she must have come off a cab rank,' said Groucho.

'What little inner voice called you to the church, *mon padre*?' said Watson.

'One day when I was young, I saw a tree, and I said to myself, "André, that's for you" – which is all very strange, because my name is François.'

'Tell me,' said Dr Watson. 'Do you flagellate?'

'No, not personally,' said the priest. 'Twice a week a Miss Rita Thighs comes in and beats the shit out of me.'

'Do religious people run in your family?' said Watson.

'Oh yes, ozerwise they would be caught.'

'Do you ever hear from the Pope?' asked Watson.

'Only when I stop sending the money,' replied the priest.

'What a two-timing religion,' said Sir Lew from inside a deep financial depression.

'Two times nothing,' said the priest. 'My father's done five bank jobs a week.' There was the wail of a police siren.

'There goes one now,' said the priest, crossing himself, and why not, he's crossed everybody else.

Rebecca improved with every moan, and the room was filled with cheering, singing and dancing, the pipes playing Paul McCartney's 'Mull of Kintyre', the farm and all the cattle stock.

'That's a hit,' said the psychiatrist, hitting the piper.

'Och,' said McGonagall in horror, putting down newspapers. 'They're wearing out the carpet and it was brand new only eighty years ago.'

'Oyyyy, my life, someone's stolen my mezuzah,' said Rebecca.

'There's been a robbery,' said an instant policeman. 'Nobody move.'

'What's he talking about?' wailed Rebecca. 'We can't afford to move.'

'I've found the mezuzah,' said Sir Lew. 'It's safe here in my bullion pocket.'

'Very well,' said the policeman. 'I declare the murder mystery of the headless corpse solved.' He twirled his truncheon round his finger. 'This is my impression of the early days of aviation,' he said.

'Ah yes,' said Dr Watson. 'I knew an early day of aviation once. He went on to become Douglas Bader, the famous legless pilot – he was never off the bottle.'

'Sacré bleu,' said the priest. 'There has been no murder here.'

'No, sir, but I have to spice up the cases because I want the promotion,' said the officer. 'For instance, that granny who stole the 50p postal order, I put that down as "The Mad Bicycle Rapist". Then the little boy who stole the scooter, I put that down as "The Bride Murdered in the Bath by the Black Strangler".'

'You're a very strange policeman, standing there in just a helmet, jock strap and boots,' said Sir Lew.

'Ah, the game is up,' said the officer, 'I'm not a constable, I'm a policeogram.' Kneeling down in front of Sir Lew he sang 'Happy Birthday to you . . .'

'Why are you singing to my groin?' said Sir Lew. 'I'm up here.'

'It's a cut-price job,' said the policeogram. 'It's twice the price standing up. Sign here.' He pointed to a cardboard cut-out.

'That was very moving,' said Sir Lew. 'Good luck in your career, which by the looks of you could be rapidly coming to an end.'

A police siren wailed.

'God, my dad is very busy today,' said le priest.

'That mezuzah,' said Rebecca, 'has been in the family since Moses crossed the Red Sea.'

The policeogram sneezed and it fell out. Dr Watson applied his stethoscope.

'I must warn you that if this goes on you could die of indecent exposure,' he said. 'Tonight there is a forecast of heavy frost which could ruin your perennials.'

'This jockstrap,' said the policeogram, 'was my mother's.'

'And it looks like she's still in it,' said Groucho. The policeogram shed a tear.

'Oh, it was only later in life that my father could tell the difference. As long as my mother wore the jockstrap and my father wore the frock, she knew she was safe.'

'Och, cheer up everybody,' said McGonagall. 'It will soon be Christmas, with a piping hot feast, with merry children and custard.'

'Lights, cameras, action,' said Sir Lew. 'If only we had them, we could make a film. I want you all at the studio, dawn tomorrow.'

'Right,' said Miss Moneypenny, spinning round in a wild dervish whirl. 'We can all stay here the night.'

'OK,' said Groucho. 'I want a door with adjoining rooms.' They all lay on the floor for the night.

Unable to sleep, McGonagall took out some sleeping pills, woke them up and swallowed them.

'I asked for adjoining rooms,' said Groucho. 'And all I got were adjoining floorboards. There's a knot in the wood and I've got a hole in the wrong place.'

'Can you keep quiet?' shouted Dr Watson.

'Yes I can,' said Groucho. 'There's a room full of it where I come from. And it's goodnight from me,' said Groucho and swallowed two earplugs.

'Thank God,' said McGonagall. 'Now we can get some sleep.'

'And while you're about it,' said Groucho. 'Run out and get me some, about six hours will do.'

McGonagall rose quietly from his bed, lit the bedside light and started to do kneebends.

'My life,' said the terrified Rebecca. 'What are you doing?'

McGonagall gave a sly grin and a wink. 'Can you no see?' he said. 'It's the Scottish foreplay.'

Rebecca crossed her leg. 'Not tonight,' she said. 'Why can't you be romantic?'

'All right,' said McGonagall. 'Would you like a fuck, darling?'

'Oh, it's no good you creeping up on me like this,' said Rebecca.

'Make up your mind lassie,' said McGonagall. 'These press-ups are killing me.'

Groucho added, 'They're killing me and I'm not even doing them.'

'This is getting us nowhere,' groaned Dr Watson.

'I didn't know we were going anywhere,' said Groucho. 'I thought we were all sleeping here.'

'One hundred and three, one hundred and four,' strained McGonagall.

'Are ye sure ye won't change your mind?'

All was quiet in the room save for the agonised crackling of McGonagall's knees.

'If I keep going, she's bound to change her mind,' he said.

'And if you keep going,' said Groucho, 'you'll have to change the sheets.' The room went quiet.

The McGonagall conjugal exercises

'One hundred and five, one hundred and six,' strained McGonagall. 'Soon they'll be nae resisting me.'

'I'll say this for you,' said Groucho. 'It's not much but I'll say this for you.'

Rebecca returned from a visit to find McGonagall face downwards on the bed.

'Oh my life, he's done it without me,' she said and fell into a deep hot salt-beef sandwich dream.

'Oh,' she groaned. 'Oh.'

'I think she's doing it by herself as well,' said Groucho. Again the room went quiet. There came a strange gurgling sound from inside the cupboard, and they knew the nude banjo player was doing terrible things to himself, but what they were the world would never know. All they knew was the cupboard was leaking, shuddering and the banjo player was hissing the word 'FISH' through the keyhole.

'By the morning,' said Groucho, 'he'll be on a white stick with a seeing eye dog and the Queen's telegram for reaching a hundred.' A strange convulsed noise came from the cupboard, ending with a hiss.

'I bet that's taken the skin off,' said Groucho.

'What are you doing in zere?' said ze French priest who had just finished one himself.

'Oooooohhhhh,' groaned McGonagall and started to poem:

Oooohhhh terrible nurgling in the night,
Which is usually done out of sight,
With strange things called swonnicles,
Supposed to be shaped like monocles.
It's something done in an empty cupboard,
Like that what was found by Old Mother Hubbard.
All night with his swonnicles he'd play,
Never giving a fig for the following day.

187

One hundred and twenty, one hundred and twenty-two,
And that should be enough for me and you.

'Och,' continued McGonagall through crackling knees
bend. 'I'm in my prime.'

'Well, stay there,' said Rebecca and fell into a deep bowl
of kosher chicken sleep. The policeogram had sung himself
to sleep with birthday greetings. The psychiatrist was
dreaming of an oven-ready turkey in a pink isosceles tri-
angle, with outboard motor attached, but then he would,
wouldn't he? For his part the French priest was dreaming of
a nun with outboard motor attached. It was a recurring
dream and here she comes again. McGonagall's fither woke
up with a start and went back to sleep with it. In the
morning all of them arrived at the studios.

The bus was stopped by a security guard, who addressed
the Nigerian driver.

> To Mrs J. Thomas Uboti,
> High Street,
> Nigeria,
> Africa.

'Now, where are you going, driver?' said the guard. The
Nigerian driver looked puzzled.

'All right,' said the security guard. 'Where am you goin'
den?'

'Dese people am making de film,' said de driver.

'What am de name of de fillum?' said the guard.

'Leave this to me,' said Dr Watson. 'Now, Mr Security
Man, you'll want some form of identification.'

'No, sir,' said the security guard. 'You do.' Dr Watson
handed it out of the window.

'I see you're a big man,' said the security guard. 'This is a
photograph of you?'

'Yes, that is a photograph of me,' said Dr Watson.

'Well, that seems to be in order,' said the guard.

'You,' said Watson. 'Can I see your photograph?'

'Certainly,' said the guard and handed him a photograph.

'This isn't you,' said Watson. 'This is a Chinaman.'

'I know sir,' said the guard. 'But I'm off-duty and he isn't. Have all these people got identity photographs?'

'Yes,' said Watson and handed him a bunch.

'These aren't photographs sir, this is just a bunch,' said the guard. 'I'll have to see their individual photographs.'

'Here you are,' said Watson obligingly.

'Wait a minute,' said the guard. 'This isn't a bunch of photographs, this is a photograph of a bunch.'

'Yes, we're Lord Grade's bunch,' said Watson.

'So,' said the guard. 'If you're Lord Grade's bunch, where's yours?'

Dr Watson gave a faraway gaze and lowered his trousers. 'My bunch are living in a little cottage on the Isle of Skye when I last saw them. They grew their own vegetables and raised turkeys.'

'I see,' said the guard. 'They were turkey raisers, were they?'

'My turkeys are too heavy to raise. They have to get up on their own.'

'Are you sure you're the security guard?' said Watson. 'I mean, look where your trousers are, they don't look very secure.'

'Oh yes, I am the security guard,' he said, pointing to his hat.

'Well, none of us feel very secure,' said Watson, pointing to *his* hat.

'Is it the Nigerian driver, sir?' said the guard. 'Only he ate one of the last lot, so if he's with you the rest of the day, don't stand near any salt or pepper pots.' The Nigerian driver went white with rage.

'Och, you're looking better,' said McGonagall, pointing to his hat.

'Am you suggestin' dat I'm eatin' de passengers?' said the driver.

'No, no, Mr Uboti,' said the security guard. 'Don't get upset. It's just that we haven't seen Des O'Connor since you drove him home.'

'One hundred and fifty, one hundred and fifty-one,' said McGonagall with his Scottish precoital press-ups.

'That's right,' said Groucho. 'He's exercising his conjugal rights and I've never seen them look better.'

'Drive on then,' said Watson patting Mr Uboti on his head. 'You're a fine-looking man and we're very proud of you. Just let me take your knife, fork and spoon. How was the last passenger?'

'Delicious,' said de driver. 'But dey am going to miss him on TV.'

Oooohhhh terrible loss of Des O'Connor,
Not seeing him on TV made me feel quite ill, your
   honour.
Being eaten by someone from Nigeria,
Who thought the meal quite inferior.
He was used to eating hippos they say,
So three cheers, hip, hip, hooray.

'Och, so,' said McGonagall. 'One day I'll be up there with Shakespeare and Byron.'

'Personally,' said Groucho. 'I can't wait for you to join them. Anybody got a shovel?'

'Will you stop digging that grave,' said McGonagall. 'I'm too young to die.'

'Nonsense,' said Groucho. 'You have all the makings of a prime corpse if ever I saw one. Just lie in that hole and leave the rest to me.'

190

'Will I need a will?' said Rebecca.

'A Will, Jim or Fred, any of those boys will do once he's dead,' said Groucho.

'Welcome to my studios,' said Sir Lew and blew a smoke ring.

'Shouldn't that be coming out of the other end?' said Watson.

'Och,' said McGonagall. 'There's a hole in your smoke. You should tell your tobacconist.'

'Don't worry,' said Sir Lew. 'I ordered them with holes in so I could see my money through it. Now, Rebecca, my love,' said Sir Lew and his money. 'Do you know what this film is going to make you?'

'Sick,' said Rebecca.

Sir Lew smiled, the effort nearly killed him. 'Rebecca, my dear, my life, my turn, do you realise you've got your foot on the first rung of the ladder of fame?'

'Och,' said McGonagall. 'That's all she's got to put on it. Have you a small part for me?'

'Yes,' said Sir Lew. 'Just stuff this cushion up your back and *voilà*.'

'So that's a *voilà*,' said Groucho. 'I always thought it was a Quasimodo.'

'No, look,' said Sir Lew, running a million pounds through his fingers. 'You'll be the new Gracie Fields.'

'She's dead,' said Rebecca.

'Yes,' said Sir Lew. 'And now it's your turn. I can see it now.'

'I wish I could,' said McGonagall. 'Perhaps I need glasses.'

'My advice to her,' said Dr Watson, 'is that she should lie down until the film starts.'

'And my advice,' said Groucho digging a second grave, 'is that she should stay there until it ends.'

'If you insult my wife, you insult me,' said McGonagall,

trying his grave for size.

'Where I come from,' said Groucho, 'that's fighting talk.'

'For Heaven's sake,' said Dr Watson, 'don't you ever stop?'

'I did once, but she got up and walked away.'

'I thought one of you was supposed to be looking for the missing Prime Minister?' said Sir Lew.

'That's perfectly true,' said McGonagall.

THE END

McGonagall escaping creditors